INVITATION TO PARADISE

INVITATION TO PARADISE

Catherine Vincent

Chivers
Bath, England

•

Thorndike Press
Waterville, Maine USA

This Large Print edition is published by BBC Audiobooks Ltd, England, and by Thorndike Press, USA.

Published in 2003 in the U.K. by arrangement with Juliet Burton Literary Agency.

Published in 2003 in the U.S. by arrangement with Juliet Burton Literary Agency.

U.K. Hardcover   ISBN 0–7540–7254–1 (Chivers Large Print)
U.S. Softcover   ISBN 0–7862–5459–9 (Nightingale Series)

The text of this Large Print edition is unabridged.
Other aspects of the book may vary from the original edition.

Set in 16 pt. New Times Roman.

Printed in Great Britain on acid-free paper.

British Library Cataloguing in Publication Data available

Library of Congress Cataloging-in-Publication Data

Vincent, Catherine, 1951–
        Invitation to paradise / by Catherine Vincent.
            p. cm.
        ISBN 0–7862–5459–9 (lg. print : sc : alk. paper)
        1. Single mothers—Fiction. 2. Hawaii—Fiction.
        3. Widows—Fiction. 4. Large type books. I. Title.
PR6072.I48I58 2003
823'.914—dc21   2003045854

CHAPTER ONE

Any illusion that it was going to be an ordinary day vanished into thin air the moment Lindsay opened her eyes. She woke to the sound of the rain drumming noisily against the bedroom window, but that wasn't what made the day unusual. She had woken up to that sound for weeks.

Winter had come early that year, after a short and chilly summer hardly worthy of calling the name. July and August had been dull and grey with scarcely a glimpse of the sun, and by the time November came round, the rain had well and truly set in.

It spattered down, day after day, in a seemingly endless torrent, and that morning was no different, except, of course, that it was. Her flat was empty of all the small, familiar things which made it home, and her cases were standing packed and waiting in the hall. Abruptly, she sat up, a shiver of anticipation feathering along her spine.

'Oh, well,' she said, 'today's the day. We're off to live in Hawaii.'

Swinging long legs elegantly out of bed, she made straight for the bathroom. A taxi was coming at seven-thirty to take them to catch their train, so a quick shower had to do, and a hasty, all-over rub left her skin glowing like a rose. Then, wrapping herself in the fleecy folds of the towel, she went into Jack's bedroom.

He was fast asleep in his cot, his chubby, three-year-old body still curled cosily under the covers. Gently, she smoothed the dark curls from his forehead, and he stirred and smiled, looking so like Jamie that her heart turned a sudden, painful somersault.

It was no wonder Jamie's mother wanted so much to see him, her beautiful grandson, the last precious link with his lost father. He was the son poor Jamie himself had never seen. Just for a moment the room was lost behind a veil of shimmering tears, and Lindsay's hand rose to her throat, trying to ease the ache that had settled there.

Dear, sweet, loving Jamie, always laughing, always so full of life. He had been her first love, her only love. They had been so young when they met, in those first few, strange weeks at university. They had known even then, they had been meant for each other.

Reserved and quieter than most girls of her age, an only child brought up by an elderly aunt, Lindsay had been shy at first of his brash, American ways. He seemed so confident, so sure of himself. But from the moment he first caught sight of her, he had been captivated by her gentle smile, her natural-born sweetness. He had eyes for no one else.

Before long they had been hopelessly, head-over-heels in love. The world seemed theirs

2

for the taking, but six months was all they'd had—six short, wonderful, glorious months.

They married at Christmas, a quiet affair with only a couple of friends at the church, but then a skidding car on a wet, June day snatched Jamie away for good, leaving Lindsay to discover about the baby alone.

Miserably, she sighed, gritting her teeth against the painful memory. She'd been left with nothing, except Jamie's child, living, growing inside her. What else could she do but pull through?

The college had helped a lot, taking her back after the birth, letting her finish her course. Now, she was back on her feet, a twenty-three-year old teacher with a fine, growing son.

'And we're doing OK, aren't we, my son?' she whispered down to the small, sleeping form.

So why was she leaving? Why was she moving away from everything she knew, everything she had worked so hard to achieve? She'd given up her job, the lease on the flat, everything. Her boats were well and truly burned.

But who could resist an invitation to paradise, even if the lawyer who'd delivered it had been hardly welcoming? She could see him now, sitting behind the table he was using as a desk, his attention riveted to the papers in front of him. He scarcely glanced up when she came into the room.

'Gardener Mitchell, the Holland family lawyer,' he stated briefly.

He was leafing through his documents, concentration etched deep on his handsome features, positively oozing authority and self assurance. There was a commanding air about him which set her teeth rather on edge. Pushy men weren't really her personal cup of tea.

Politely, she took a seat, waiting for him to look-up, but when the silence stretched on and on, for what seemed like hours in the quiet room, Lindsay thought the time had come. If he wouldn't speak, then she would.

'I'm Lindsay Holland,' she introduced herself.

'Pleased to meet you,' he replied, looking up at last and throwing her a brief, smooth smile.

Everything about the man was dark—the wavy hair, the straight black brows, the Californian-type tan, so it came as something of a surprise to meet such a pair of deep blue eyes in so very bronzed a setting. Those same blue eyes were looking over at her, brows raised, regarding her now with a faint speculation darkening their cool depths.

'You call yourself Mrs Holland?' he enquired at last.

His tone was courtesy itself, but nevertheless, she had the distinct feeling he didn't really approve.

4

'Jamie and I were married,' she said. 'What else should I call myself?'

For a moment his eyes rested on her upturned countenance, then he gave a shrug of those powerful shoulders.

'Nothing else, Mrs Holland,' he acceded with a second careful smile.

Presenting a façade of polite good manners became increasing difficult under his watchful gaze. Seconds passed, and he didn't move, didn't speak, and Lindsay began to seriously wonder if he was doing it on purpose, just to put her at some sort of disadvantage. Despite his film star good looks, she couldn't really say she liked the man, but courtesy prevented her from letting him see it.

Let him say what he had to say, she told herself. It wasn't as if she'd asked for this meeting. She had never approached Jamie's family, even when Jack had been born. The request to see him had come solely from them, or rather, from Jamie's mother, Eleanor Holland.

'You understand, of course, that I'm acting for Eleanor Holland,' Gardener Mitchell said at last, and when she nodded, he continued smoothly, 'and it's my job to make sure her interests are protected.'

'Interests?'

She hadn't the vaguest notion what he meant, and his eyes narrowed fractionally at her bemused expression.

'Interests,' he insisted softly. 'Mrs Holland is a very wealthy woman, and Jamie was her only child. I'm here to see that her generosity isn't abused, to make sure she isn't hurt or taken advantage of.'

The silence in the room was deafening as the light finally dawned in Lindsay's head. Her eyes flew to his, widened in shocked disbelief as the significance of the words fully sank in.

'You mean me, don't you?' she broke in, her voice chilled beyond freezing point. 'You think I'm cheating her, that Jack isn't really her grandson!'

Gardener Mitchell took one look at her stunned features, and he raised a horrified hand.

'Good heavens, I didn't mean that,' he exclaimed. 'We know Jack is Jamie's son. The likeness is too great for anything else, even in a photograph.'

'Then what?' she challenged, with scarcely a trace less ice in her tone.

Suddenly, she didn't trust him an inch. But at least he'd stopped short of the ultimate outrage. He wasn't trying to deny her son his parentage.

'I just wanted to make sure you intended to stay around for a time,' he informed her calmly. 'If you do come to the islands, don't be in so much of a hurry to leave Eleanor's establishment. Let her feel she has a part in Jack's life, an important part.'

6

He didn't believe in pulling his punches, did he? Now he thought she was out for what she could get!

'What are you saying?' she demanded, aghast. 'You think I'll use Jack to get what I want and then leave?'

Gardener Mitchell's eyes never left her face, their expression veiled, but at least he smiled at her.

'I'm sorry if my comments have upset you,' he declared, 'but they had to be said. Eleanor is very vulnerable at the moment, and you are a stranger.'

'That doesn't make me dishonest,' she snapped back.

'Perhaps not,' he agreed, 'but I am her lawyer. I have to make sure.'

Grudgingly, she shrugged. Perhaps he was right. But he could have been a bit more tactful about it.

'Eleanor is Jamie's mother, I could never do anything to hurt her,' she began, trying to make him understand.

'Good,' he cut in. 'I'm so glad to hear it. Then you won't mind sharing your son with her.'

Lindsay paused, throwing him a questioning look. What could he possibly mean by that?

'Share Jack?' she countered. 'Of course I intend to share him. Isn't that the whole idea of a family?'

At once he rose to his feet, collecting his

papers from the table in front of him with a meticulous smile.

'Absolutely,' he agreed.

Lindsay hadn't seen him again, and she couldn't say she was exactly sorry. That evening he'd flown back to the islands, and within days, the airline tickets had dropped on her doormat, inviting her to visit Eleanor. It didn't enter her head for a moment not to accept. This was Jamie's mother, Jack's grandmother. She could hardly wait to meet her.

Suddenly, Jack stirred and stretched, bringing Lindsay abruptly back to the present. He was the real reason, of course, the reason for moving. She had no family left, no one but herself to offer.

Eleanor Holland could offer Jack roots, the security of a family, a knowledge of his place in life. How could she possibly deny him that?

Jamie's mother was right. Their home wasn't here any more. Their home was with her, thousands of miles away on the paradise island of Oahu.

With a faint snore, the little boy rolled over, settling again without waking, and she smiled at the snuffling, animal sound.

'No more cold, wet winters for you,' she promised, leaving his side to pad back to her own room.

She'd chosen trousers to travel in, slim and smart in dark blue, teaming them with a fluid jade top. Taller than average and as slender as a wand, Lindsay was without doubt what most people would consider a beautiful woman. Wide brown eyes fringed with thick, dark lashes of a quite exceptional length gazed solemnly out from a face that needed little makeup to enhance its beauty.

It was framed by a waterfall of long golden hair, tumbling about her shoulders. Quickly, she caught it into a loose bunch at the nape of her neck with a narrow satin ribbon, smoothing any loose tendrils carefully over her ears. That way, it would be easier to keep tidy while they were travelling.

The clock in the hall chimed. It was time to get Jack out of bed, and they had breakfast together in the half-empty kitchen, pretending it was a picnic. Then she got him washed and dressed in record time.

'We're going to see Grandma today,' she said, threading his arms into the sleeves of his new red jacket.

'In a aeroplane,' he added, wide-eyed.

Getting herself and a small boy onto a flight at Heathrow, not to mention all her luggage, wasn't something she was exactly looking forward to, but train rides were still something of a novelty for Jack, so he was fairly engrossed as far as the airport. Even at the airport itself, things went better than she expected. With a toddler in tow and first-class tickets in her hand, they were ushered on to the aircraft almost at once.

From there on, it developed into quite the most exhausting journey Lindsay had ever had. They were in the air for hours without a break, and she didn't get much chance to rest. Jack was a live wire and being cooped up inside, even the thrill of flying began to lose its interest.

At Los Angeles they went through customs, but mercifully Jack was tired by then, and he slept through most of the formalities. Once they were back on the aircraft, she didn't hear another peep out of him.

At long last, she had a moment to herself, and she settled back in her seat, determined to take advantage of it. Thankfully, she closed her eyes, and she'd almost drifted off when the warm North American accent of the stewardess broke abruptly into her reverie, announcing their journey's end.

At once, her eyes were drawn to the window. Scattered far below lay a carpet of blazing lights, all glittering and winking like multi-coloured jewels in the indigo velvet night.

'Honolulu,' she said, breathlessly.

They had reached Hawaii at last.

Jack was still lost to the world, sleeping against her shoulder as they alighted. He was a dead weight, and giving a small sigh, she shifted him into a more comfortable position. But at least it gave her the chance to catch her first glimpse of the island. Palm trees, touched by the very lightest of ocean breezes, stretched tall against a magical night sky rich with a thousand stars, and she took a deep breath, filling her head with the spicy aroma.

She joined the flow of fellow passengers and was swept along in the crowd towards the departures lounge. She'd been told a car would be there to meet her, and she scanned the floor for the sign of a driver's uniform. But there wasn't a soul even vaguely matching that description.

Around her, the crowds were gradually thinning out, but there was still no glimpse of a uniform. Then her eyes finally alighted on a male figure pushing his way through the door. Wearily, she closed her eyes. But he was still there when she opened them. Why, she thought, of all the people in the world, did it have to be him?

Tall and commanding, his eyes looking over the thinning crowds, it was the lawyer, Gardener Mitchell. He pushed through the remaining peole with scarcely an effort. They just seemed to melt away in front of him, and Lindsay had to admit, the man had an air about him, a demeanour that gave the distinct impression of authority. He was obviously used to giving orders, rather than ever taking them.

Somehow, she managed to compose her features into a welcoming smile. It wasn't much, but it was the best she could manage under the circumstances. She couldn't pretend she liked the man.

'Good evening, Mr Mitchell,' she ventured as he approached. 'I didn't expect to be met by anyone quite so exalted.'

'Eleanor wouldn't trust you to anyone else,' he returned smoothly.

She put out her free hand, still determined to be polite, but he didn't take it. Strong, brown fingers reached out of nowhere to cup her chin, tilting her face up towards him. Lindsay froze in sheer disbelief. The man was intending to kiss her! Powerless to do a single thing to prevent it, all she could do was stand and wait, her body held ramrod straight as his mouth descended to brush her cheek.

'What are you doing?' she began, but he waved the words aside.

'Aloha, Mrs Holland,' he said, slipping a sweet-smelling garland of blossoms over her head. 'I hope you don't mind the traditional island welcome. No one ever arrives in Hawaii without receiving a lei of flowers and a kiss, so it was up to me to do the honours.'

'Er . . . yes, of course,' she stammered back, caught completely off guard.

Momentarily, she was caught at a loss for words, and she chewed her bottom lip in exasperated silence. What on earth was the matter with her, blushing and bridling and imagining the worst like some silly schoolgirl? And with Gardener Mitchell, of all people, the coldest fish she knew. Thank goodness she'd stopped short of slapping his face!

Without another word, he collected her cases, and she stood back, giving her flushed cheeks a chance to cool. The man was still a might high-handed for her taste, but she let him get on with it. Fatigue was catching up with her fast, and her feet felt like lead, not to mention Jack, who seemed to be getting heavier with every step. Gently, she shifted him over a little, easing the weight on her shoulder.

'Here we are.'

Gardener Mitchell indicated the kind of long, gleaming saloon Lindsay had previously thought only existed in American television programmes. She said nothing as he flung open the door, but one glance inside and she had to smile. There was a chid's car seat in the back, looking particularly incongruous perched amid all that luxury.

'Eleanor insisted on it, for her precious grandson,' he explained.

He took the sleeping child from her, and she watched unprotesting as he fastened the little boy safely in place. She was too weary to argue, and besides, he seemed to know what he was doing.

Perhaps, she wondered idly, the man had small children of his own. Though, to be honest, she thought, he didn't seem the domesticated type.

'Ready to go now?' he asked, holding wide the passenger door, and nodding, she slipped inside.

Silently, he slid into the seat beside her, saying nothing as he guided the car into the stream of fast-moving traffic leaving the airport.

'Is it far?' she queried as the lights of Honolulu fell behind them.

'Some way,' he confirmed. 'The Holland estate is up country, on the island's windward shore. Though,' he added, a touch apologetically, 'you won't see much of the place in the dark.'

She felt he expected a reply. With a show of polite interest, she nodded.

'I'm looking forward to seeing the islands,' she ventured.

He lapsed into silence again, his eyes on the road ahead, and left to herself, Lindsay couldn't resist the opportunity to sneak a brief, sideways look at the man at her side.

Clearly dressed for dinner in an exquisitely tailored white suit that fitted his tall figure like a glove, he was certainly worth a second glance.

In his mid-thirties and drop dead gorgeous, if you happened to like men without a drop of red blood in their veins. The man was far too much of a stuffed shirt for her taste. Work and success, lots of success, were all he cared about, she hazarded to guess. His profile was

14

still staring strictly ahead so she risked another look, much longer than the first, her eyes half hidden beneath a dark fringe of carefully lowered lashes.

Power, wealth and good looks, Gardener Mitchell certainly had them all a pretty lethal combination for most women. Some women, she corrected herself quickly. To her, men like Gardener Mitchell were eminently resistible.

'Not much farther now,' his voice intruded suddenly into her ear, catching her mid-thought. 'We should be there soon.'

The countryside swept past without a single light to relieve it. When the vehicle pulled suddenly to a halt, it was the last thing she was expecting.

'Are we here?' she asked, peering doubtfully into what appeared to be nothing but total darkness. 'I can't see a house.'

'You won't,' her companion returned smoothly. 'We're not there yet. I thought you might like to see the ocean before we go in.'

He was right again. No matter how tired she was, Lindsay couldn't wait to see the Pacific at close hand. She virtually fell out of the car, gazing hopefully into the darkness. The highway ran right along the edge of the shore, and she could see it clearly, the surf white and gleaming against a pale shimmer of sand. At once, she took a few hasty steps towards it.

'Careful,' his voice called after her, 'it's very dark.'

He couldn't have said a truer word. Above her, the night sky was strewn with more stars than Lindsay had ever believed existed.

'If you look carefully,' he said, 'you can see the Southern Cross.'

He pointed to a starry configuration low on the horizon, and with a faint start, Lindsay suddenly realised how close he was standing. Frowning, she concentrated hard on the horizon, but it was no good. The Southern Cross might be right under her nose, but there was no way she was going to find it. All she could think of was Gardener Mitchell.

'Is something the matter?' he queried, sensing the uncertainty quivering through the slender body beside him.

'I don't think I'm looking in the right place,' she managed at last.

She would never let on it was him making her feel so strange, and she lifted her head to look at him. But the features gazing down into hers were lost in shadow, their expression unseen.

'Actually,' he admitted slowly, his voice no more than a whisper in the silence, 'I had another reason for stopping here before we reach the estate.'

Whatever he had to say to her, she could guess it wasn't going to be good. But pride held her shoulders straight and her head erect. Her heart might be fighting to beat double time under her ribs, but he would never guess he was the reason for it.

'Oh, yes?' she returned quietly, but he didn't reply at once.

Frowning, he looked down at her, finally seeming to see the exhausted eyes and the soft droop to her mouth.

'I'm so sorry,' he exclaimed, his tone abruptly contrite. 'You must be exhausted from your journey. Please, let me help you back to the car.'

For some strange reason her legs didn't appear to belong to her any more, so Lindsay didn't demur when he took her arm in a powerful hand. Gripping her firmly by the elbow, she allowed him to lead her back, and she sank thankfully into the sumptuous upholstery as he restarted the car. But he made no effort to move away.

Lindsay felt her nerves beginning to tighten again. What was it he found so difficult to say? Something had to be wrong.

'Jamie's mother . . .' she began, her tone sharpened with sudden fear.

'Can't wait to meet you you,' he finished at once.

She sank back in her seat, silenced, but not entirely reassured by his words. Even in the dark interior of the car, she could see his brows were knitted, the chiselled mouth straight and unsmiling. His expression was far too severe to offer her any comfort.

'So?' she prompted.

There was no point in beating about the bush. If something was wrong, she might as well know it sooner rather than later.

His frown deepened, the handsome features set in granite, and against her will, Lindsay took a short, apprehensive breath.

'Please tell me,' she stammered.

'Very well,' he shrugged. 'There's no way I want to upset you again, but there are things I have to say.'

He didn't get any further. Anger took hold of her. Was he daring to doubt her motives again?

'Please don't start warning me off,' she snapped. 'Believe me, I have no intention of letting Eleanor down.'

For a brief moment, he didn't reply. Then one eyebrow rose, and his features assumed an expression of surprised enquiry.

'Aren't you being overly sensitive, Mrs Holland?' he asked at last. 'Is it so very remiss of me to have a word, a quiet word before we arrive, for Eleanor's sake?'

She sat very still and stared silently out of the window, unwilling to be mollified. What the man had implied was hateful. Did he expect her to forget it so soon?

'Perhaps not,' she said, slim shoulders shrugging.

His handsome features softened somewhat.

'I'm sorry,' he began. 'Maybe I didn't do this very well.'

Maybe? That was the understatement of the year! If he'd intended the worst possible insult, he couldn't have done any better.

But wearily, Lindsay waved a dismissive hand. He hadn't sounded particularly sorry but at least he'd conceded something, and perhaps he was right. She was tired, anxious, confused. Perhaps she had overreacted.

'Do go on,' she invited.

He paused once more for a moment, before taking up his narrative again.

'Well,' he began, 'Eleanor's husband, Jamie's father, was much older than her. He was my father's oldest friend.'

'Really?' Lindsay broke in, rather at a loss to where this family history was heading.

'So,' he continued, 'Eleanor is rather more than a client to me. She is a dear friend as well.'

Lindsay was still mystified. Why was he telling her all this?

'Then you're close,' she acceded carefully.

'Very close,' he confirmed. 'So, contrary to what you might think, I really couldn't have been happier when we discovered Jamie had a son. When you agreed to bring him to Oahu, it gave Eleanor a new interest in life, a reason for living. After losing Ray first, then Jamie, all in the same year,' he persisted, his handsome features dark, 'I thought for a time that she wouldn't get over it.'

Lindsay closed her eyes against the

19

bleakness of his expression and her throat constricted painfully. Poor Eleanor, bereft and desperately alone, losing everything she loved in just a few short months. What would she have felt, if it had happened to her, if she had lost Jack as well as Jamie?

A tremor ran through her, as cold as ice, chilling the blood in her veins. It didn't bear thinking about.

'I can imagine,' she said.

But there was more. She could see it in the straight line of his mouth, in the watchful eyes searching hers.

'But you didn't stop here just to tell me this,' she added quietly.

'You're right,' he admitted, 'there is more. Emotionally, Eleanor is still very frail, and sadly, her health is also far from robust. She couldn't survive another loss. She needs stability, care and all the support we can give.'

There was only one answer to that, and Lindsay gave it automatically.

'Anything I can do, I will,' she insisted, as if he needed to ask!

Staring up, she met narrowed, blue eyes that seemed to pin her to her seat. Did he still not trust her, the wretched man?

'You're sure?' he queried, his voice insistent.

'Positive,' she answered back, head high.

'Good,' he replied. 'So Eleanor will be in safe hands.'

Eleanor again, she noted. Is that what all this was about? Was there really more than friendship between Gardener Mitchell and Jamie's mother?

For a brief moment, Lindsay felt strangely loath to follow the notion through. The thought of the disapproving lawyer being constantly in the background, watching her every move, looking down his superior nose at her, wasn't really her idea of fun but she had to face facts.

Wearily, Lindsay closed her eyes, trying to bring her unwilling thoughts back into some sort of order.

'Oh, dear,' she muttered to herself, 'isn't that just my luck? I've come halfway round the world to start a new life, only to be stuck with Gardener Mitchell breathing down my neck all the time!'

CHAPTER TWO

'Mrs Holland, are you all right?' Gardener Mitchell said, breaking into Lindsay's thoughts, and she nodded quickly, biting her lip.

She had the instinctive feeling that he had already considered all the options, and was carefully manipulating things his way. The man had got what he wanted.

'I don't need watching,' she reminded him bleakly.

'Relax, my dear,' he said, turning hooded blue eyes towards her. 'We're on the same side, Eleanor's side.'

The words were intended to be reassuring, but the man was so used to having his own way. Could she ever cross swords with him and survive the experience? Finally, to her relief, he took hold of the wheel again, and the car pulled away. It turned almost at once through open wrought-iron gates, moving down a long, broad drive beneath a canopy of leafy trees.

Minutes later, it rolled to a standstill in front of a large, white house. Lights were blazing across a broad veranda, illuminating the sweeping flight of steps leading up to the front door.

'Kahana House, the Holland family home,' Gardener Mitchell announced, waving a hand towards the magnificent façade.

Open-mouthed, Lindsay climbed out of the car. She had known that Jamie's family was wealthy, of course, but it had never really occurred to her how sumptuous their lifestyle might be. It did now, with a vengeance, as she caught her first sight of Kahana House.

Even half-concealed by the velvety darkness, the place took her breath away. Built in colonial style, its walls painted a dazzling white, the main house was long and low with a green tiled roof and huge windows running from ceiling to floor. The veranda extended around its entire outer edge, giving a shady place to sit and take tea in the hottest part of the day.

'It must have a dozen bedrooms at least,' she commented, gazing up at its sweeping lines. It was a fairly accurate guess. Ten bedrooms were actually nearer the truth, with half a dozen bathrooms and a whole series of elegant living-rooms gracing the ground floor.

'Shall we go in?' her companion invited.

He had extricated Jack from his seat, but Lindsay didn't want him carrying her child inside, not when they first met Eleanor. That was her privilege. Quickly, she took the boy into her own arms.

'I thought you were tired,' he began.

'I can manage now,' she assured him.

He strode ahead, and she followed in silence. Only moments after he rang the bell,

23

the door was opened by a middle-aged woman with greying hair smoothed into a bun. Her simple blue dress was smart and immaculate, and she smiled in greeting.

'Mr Garde,' she said. 'Come in, madam is expecting you.'

Garde, Lindsay noted. It was an unusual abbreviation. It suited him down to the ground.

'Good, good,' he responded with a smile of his own, evidently quite at home in his impressive surroundings. 'Lindsay,' he added, smoothly using her Christian name, 'this is Marsha, she runs the house for Eleanor.'

'You must be Mr Jamie's young wife, from England,' the woman broke in, her eyes misting over. 'Come in, my dear. Madam is expecting you.'

Lindsay was ushered into a magnificent entrance hall. Its coolness was welcome after the heat of the night, the walls a pale blue-green, like watered taffeta. A circular rug of muted Chinese silks covered the parquet floor. Island masks in carved wood adorned the walls, and there were plants on every available surface. Their glossy leaves and jewel-like flowers spilled down from alcoves and shelves, filling the whole place with the sweet scent of the tropics.

'This way,' Marsha urged.

Lindsay was whisked across the hall, through ceiling-high double doors.

'Lindsay, my dear.'

In one fluid movement, a woman rose from the depths of a chair opposite, her hands raised in greeting. Although she had only set eyes on her once before, in a photograph, Lindsay knew at once who it was.

'Eleanor,' she said, smiling through a tremulous mist of tears.

Small and slender, her ash blonde hair crowning her well-shaped head like a silvery cap, Eleanor was even more beautiful in the flesh. Her make-up was perfect, every hair on her head immaculately groomed, and a dress in palest blue draped her slim figure in designer elegance.

Lindsay lost count of the times she was hugged, her head filled with the delicate scent of Eleanor's perfume, her body enveloped in the woman's soft arms. Then Jack was snatched away, and covered in such a flurry of kisses he was quite overwhelmed.

His lips started to tremble, but before Lindsay could reach him, Eleanor had rung the bell and a young woman came promptly into the room.

'Be a good boy,' Eleanor said gently, handing him into the woman's arms, 'and let Chrissie take you to bed. Mummy will be there in a moment, when she's had a little rest.'

'A nanny?' Lindsay exclaimed. 'I've always looked after Jack myself.'

'And so you still shall,' Eleanor's soothing

response came. 'But you won't mind a little help, will you?'

Unable to come up with an adequate reason that sounded even vaguely logical, words caught momentarily in Lindsay's throat. But logic had nothing to do with it. She had always put Jack to bed herself, since the day he'd been born, and the thought of handing over that precious time to a nanny tore her to shreds.

'Of course Lindsay won't mind,' Garde broke in, answering for her.

She shook her head. Oh well, I suppose it won't hurt, just for this evening, she comforted herself, watching her son disappear through the doors in the arms of the smiling girl.

Tired herself, she longed for her own bed. Seventeen hours without sleep was enough to finish anyone, to say nothing of the jetlag that was beginning to plague her. But Eleanor had poured them all a drink of chilled champagne to celebrate their safe arrival, so an early escape was out of the question.

Minutes passed as Lindsay sat politely on the edge of her chair, slowly sipping her drink. Her eyes were aching abominably, not to mention the rest of her body, and her conversation definitely began to dwindle.

Eleanor, though, wanted to talk about Jamie, and she turned to Lindsay, her eyes bright with unshed tears.

'His journal came back, with the other

belongings,' she said, 'but it was months before I could bring myself to read it. Then I found out about you.'

'We met at college, in the first week,' Lindsay began to explain.

'And you made him so happy,' Eleanor finished for her.

An ache began in Lindsay's throat and she swallowed convulsively, barely managing to keep her own tears at bay. These were poignant, bittersweet memories they were stirring.

'We were both happy,' she breathed.

'I know,' Eleanor agreed. 'His diaries . . . he wrote a lot about you.'

She sighed, and a vague, formless fear suddenly clutched at Lindsay's heart. Eleanor looked almost too fragile for words, her skin stretched like fine tissue paper over her high cheekbones, her eyes too dark in her pale face. This woman was ill, far more ill than Garde had admitted to her.

Immediately, his voice broke into the silence, reassuring and soft.

'But we have Jack,' he said gently, soothing away her pain. 'Jamie would have loved him.'

Eleanor paused, still silent, but a faint, tremulous curve touched her lips.

'Adored him, you mean,' she corrected, her expression growing tender. 'He would have been so proud, and I want to make sure Jack has everything he would have had if his father

27

had still been with us. I want to make him my heir.'

'But you've done enough already,' Lindsay interrupted, startled.

Make Jack her heir? What did that mean? The boy needed a family, that was for sure, and he needed to know something about his father. But Eleanor's heir? It was a notion she'd never really considered.

'Of course,' Eleanor continued, her voice taking on a brisk, no-nonsense tone. 'I've made up my mind. Jack will have everything I can give him.'

Dazed, Lindsay shook her head. A feeling of cold disbelief washed over her, and the struggle to keep the smile on her face was almost too much to manage. She drew in a deep breath, then another, fighting to keep her voice suitably light.

'Maybe we can talk about it some other time,' she began.

'There's nothing to talk about,' Eleanor returned. 'My dear, Jack is Jamie's son. We can't deny him his inheritance. I must adopt him officially into the family. Garde did assure me you were prepared to share.'

The sound of those soft words tore the breath straight from Lindsay's body. She had no idea how long she stood there, wide-eyed, stunned into silence, wondering if she'd heard them correctly.

'Eleanor,' Garde's voice intruded at last,

chiding her gently, 'I really think Lindsay has heard enough for one day. Maybe we should let her retire to her room. We can discuss things like this some other time.'

His eyes, resting on Eleanor, were soft with affection. But they narrowed slightly as they slid Lindsay's way, darkened with silent warning.

'Yes,' Lindsay whispered.

There was absolutely nothing else she could think of to say, not unless she gave way to screaming hysterics! Then Garde rose, his silent presence at Eleanor's side another subtle warning.

'Of course,' Eleanor's voice tinkled again into the room, 'we have all the time in the world,' she added. 'I'm having a get-together on the beach, as soon as you're ready for it. Nothing formal, you know, just a small gathering to introduce you and Jack to all my friends.'

'It sounds wonderful,' Lindsay murmured dutifully, though she had the distinct feeling it was Jack who mattered, but fatigue had finally edged into her voice, and Eleanor threw her a sudden, sympathetic look.

'Oh, my dear,' she said at once, her hands rising upwards in a flutter of loving concern, 'we must get you to bed. Garde is right. We can talk all about it tomorrow.'

She rang immediately for Marsha, and Lindsay followed the housekeeper thankfully

29

to her room. It was spacious and airy like the rest of the house, a vision of cut glass, white carpet and pale, polished wood. But it was the king-size bed which caught Lindsay's eye. It looked deep and welcoming, with the softest of pale pink covers.

First, though, she had to check on Jack, and she pushed open the adjoining door. Her son was asleep in the kind of nursery suite she had only ever set eyes on in films, sharing a little blue bed with the largest teddy bear she had ever seen. For one crazy moment she felt like grabbing their clothes and running like mad. But where would she go? She was too far from home to run. Tremulously, she smiled down at the small, sleeping child, leaving him to dream on.

With a sigh, she discarded her clothes and stepped into the bathroom. Tired or not, she turned the shower full on, emerging a few minutes later, clean and glowing, to pull a shortie nightdress in coolest cotton over her dampened hair. Moonlight was filtering in through the tall windows, bathing the room in silver, and she left the curtains wide, drawn back in their long, tasselled ties.

The bed was waiting and Lindsay climbed in. But sleep was slow in coming. Blindly, she stared up at the ceiling, seeing nothing but Jamie's smiling face, clear in every single detail, and her throat ached with the effort of holding back the tears. He would have known what to do, about Jack, about Eleanor. She wanted their son to have opportunities, of course. She wanted him to have a good life. But all he needed was love. There was no need for Eleanor to rush into anything else.

Is this what Garde meant when he'd talked about sharing her son? Adoption? He surely couldn't imagine she'd ever agree to that. Jack was her son, her baby. She would never give him up. Sharing him with Eleanor was one thing, she would willingly manage that, but anything more simply wasn't an option.

She woke just after dawn the following day, her body clock still attuned to time half a world away. But she knew where she was the instant she opened her eyes. Around her, the house lay hushed and still. At a guess, no one else was even awake, but she couldn't just lie there, not with the sun streaming in through the windows, begging her to look outside.

Quickly tossing aside the covers, she rose to her feet. A robe of pale blue silk was thrown negligently over the nearest chair, but she ignored it, padding barefoot across the velvety carpet. Outside, a beautiful morning beckoned. Quietly, she turned the key in the lock, and pushed open the french doors. The sweet scent of the early day flooded into the room and Lindsay took a deep breath, sniffing appreciatively. A narrow, sunlit balcony looked out over a sandy curve of bay fringed by clusters of whispering palms, and impulsively, she stepped outside.

Before her stretched the shimmering expanse of the Pacific, a vista of turquoise waters tumbling in along the whitest of tropical beaches, deserted except for the occasional swooping gull.

So, this was Jamie's home. He had walked on that beach as a child, swum in those waves, lived, laughed, grown into a man. Her mind drifted, to a private place filled with bittersweet images of other times, other places. For a very long time she stood on the little balcony, quietly breathing in the fragrant air, her elbows resting on the white filigree ironwork.

'Good morning, Lindsay. Enjoying the view?'

Lindsay was caught mid-thought. It was Eleanor's voice, but it took a moment or two to locate her sitting below, alone on the shady veranda.

'I'm sorry, did I disturb you?' she ventured with a tiny frown.

Eleanor shook her silvery head, and she shaded her eyes, looking upward, an indulgent smile curving her lips.

'Of course not,' she said. 'Why don't you get dressed and come down? Join me for breakfast.'

Quickly, Lindsay went inside and dressed. One of her new dresses was waiting, ready to slip over her head. She touched her face lightly with make-up and caught her hair into a cool bunch at the nape of her neck.

Jack's bed was already empty. One quick peek into his room was enough to tell her that. Wryly, she shook her head, following the sound of splashing and giggling into the adjoining bathroom.

' 'Morning, Mummy,' he called out, waving his arms and blowing her a breathy kiss through the cap of bubbles covering his dark head.

' 'Morning, baby,' she grinned, dropping a kiss on his upturned face.

'I'll bring him through as soon as he's dressed,' the young nanny said, glancing up with huge, smiling eyes.

'That might take some time,' Lindsay commented wryly, judging by the amount of water splashed on the floor.

She hovered a little while longer, paused in the doorway, still smiling over at them. They seemed to be having such a good time. But Eleanor was waiting for her, ready to eat breakfast. So she sighed, reluctantly leaving them to their games, and went downstairs alone.

Eleanor was glancing through the morning paper, its pages spread out in front of her, but she looked up the moment Lindsay came into the room.

'Come and sit with me,' she invited, patting the seat beside her.

Marsha did them proud. As if by magic, hot pancakes with lashings of maple syrup and some truly delicious coffee appeared on the table. Lindsay hadn't realised she was so hungry, and she noted ruefully that Eleanor had hardly managed a thing, while she was starting into her second helping.

'It's the sea air,' Eleanor consoled, adding fresh cream from a silver jug to the delicate china cups.

Jack appeared about halfway through the meal, smelling sweetly of soap and baby powder. He came skipping into the room, rosy face alert, looking so like his father. Lindsay's heart turned over just to see him. Who on earth could blame Eleanor for falling in love with him?

'Jack,' she began, starting to rise out of her seat.

'Come and give your grandmother a big kiss,' Eleanor interrupted, arms outstretched, and the child rose obediently on tip-toe to place a huge, smacking kiss on her cheek. 'Now sit here by me,' she continued, 'and tell me all your plans for today.'

'Chrissie says we can play on the beach after breakfast,' he informed her solemnly, his eyes round and hopeful, and turning to Lindsay, he enquired with a winning smile, 'is that all right, Mummy?'

'I don't see why not,' Eleanor put in before Lindsay could so much as open her mouth.

34

'Mummy's still very tired. A quiet time to herself before the party seems a good idea to me.'

Time to herself? Lindsay swallowed hard. Who said she wanted time to herself? For a fleeting moment, she wrestled the urge to deny she wanted any such thing, then she sighed. Why not? It was early days yet. Eleanor meant well. Give it time, she promised herself. They would soon come to understand each other.

'Sounds OK to me,' she agreed with a smile.

Chrissie helped Jack to cereal and juice, then settled back to enjoy her own meal. With her brief shorts, her chatter, and her bright, swift smiles, she wasn't like any nanny Lindsay had ever imagined. As it turned out, she was right. The girl chattered non-stop over breakfast, confiding that she was a niece of Gardener Mitchell's, giving Eleanor a helping hand before she took up a college place in the autumn.

'I want to be a teacher,' Chrissie confided.

'Like me,' Lindsay told her.

'Yes, yes,' Chrissie's enthusiasm was evident. 'Maybe we can talk . . .'

'But at some other time,' Eleanor broke in, lifting a delicate hand to her pale brow. 'Go now, child, and take Jack on to the beach. All this chatter is making my head ache.'

'Sorry, Aunt Eleanor.'

Unperturbed, Chrissie took Jack's hand and led him away from the table, throwing them both a huge smile.

'See you later,' she called back.

'She's a sweet girl,' Eleanor observed, watching the two disappear towards the beach. 'But,' she added, sighing, 'so young, so full of life.'

Not that much younger than me, Lindsay reflected briefly, no more than two or three years at the most. But Eleanor was right. She felt worlds away from Chrissie.

Marsha appeared when breakfast was finished to clear the table, and Eleanor moved towards a group of deeply-cushioned garden chairs set at the edge of the veranda. She indicated for Lindsay to follow, and together they settled back in the warm, early-morning shade.

The air conditioner was humming softly to itself in the background, keeping the rooms at the same comfortable temperature. But apart from that, the house lay utterly silent, drowsing peacefully under the morning sun.

Lindsay might have drowsed herself, but the sound of her son's little voice, piping up happily with Chrissie, kept her attention more or less focused. She could see his small figure on the beach, carefully building a castle in the sand, complete with turrets and sweeping battlements.

Sighing, she eased herself more comfortably into the cushions. It was all quite perfect, the golden stillness of the morning, the scent of frangipani hanging sweetly in the air. Then suddenly, like a wasp buzzing round at a picnic, the sound of a car coming towards the drive intruded into her thoughts, and she squinted, frowning, towards it.

Oh, no, she thought, I might have known something would spoil things. Or rather, someone. It was that man, the enigmatic Gardener Mitchell. Had he come to keep his eye on her already?

He came striding up the steps with a nod and a smile, sure of his welcome, his glance searching out Eleanor. But Lindsay was quite certain those compelling blue eyes hadn't missed her sitting there.

'Eleanor,' he called out, moving towards her and catching the narrow hand in his own, immediately lifting it to his lips.

Accepting the offer of coffee, he sipped it carefully as he lounged at ease in his chair, his long legs stretched out in front of him. His attention lay purely with Eleanor, so it was easy for Lindsay to sit back, taking no part in the conversation. Surreptitiously, she watched him at work, dark lashes lowered over grave grey eyes. Talking to Eleanor, his smile ready, his blue eyes flashing with humour, he looked everyone's idea of a well-educated, professional man, his well-toned body clad in immaculate suiting of palest grey, relaxing at his ease. Charm was oozing from every pore.

Suddenly, he laughed, leaning forward,

launching into some amusing anecdote, and Eleanor's response was immediate. She glowed, putting out a hand to touch his shoulder, her pale features taking on a luminous sheen. Lindsay couldn't miss the implied intimacy. The feeling between them was more than obvious. Good grief, she sighed, does that mean I have to pretend I like the man?

'So, Lindsay, are you looking forward to your life in the islands?'

Garde's voice broke suddenly into her thoughts, politely, awaiting her answer. Thrown by her sudden inclusion in a conversation which up until then had been rolling unheeded over her head, she opened her mouth but no sound emerged. Surprise had rendered her temporarily speechless.

'Oh, dear,' Eleanor put in, 'I think Lindsay's mind was elsewhere.'

'Really?' he said, subjecting Lindsay to a second thorough appraisal, one black brow raised, but she positively refused to be flustered, meeting those watchful blue eyes with surprising equanimity.

'I'm sorry,' she countered, finding her voice at last, 'but Eleanor's right. I was miles away. Now if you'll excuse me,' she added, rising to her feet, 'I think I'll go and join Jack on the beach.'

'But I'm sure Chrissie can manage,' Eleanor started to protest.

'I'm sure she can,' Lindsay returned lightly, 'but it's a lovely day. I quite fancy a walk on the beach.'

Already, she was halfway across the veranda, heading for the steps down to the beach. Garde's eyes hadn't faltered. She could feel them still, fixed on her retreating form, disturbingly cool and direct, and with her head defiantly high in the air, she started down the steps. Sadly she was just a little too fast in her eagerness to get away.

Halfway down the flight, she felt her foot slip underneath her, catching her suddenly off balance. With a muffled shriek, she threw up her hands, clutching wildly into mid-air, but there wasn't a thing she could do to save herself. She felt herself fall, flat on her face, on to the sun-drenched beach.

The breath was knocked clean out of her body, and she lay at the foot of the steps like a rag doll, her head pillowed in the hot sand. Immediately, the sound of footsteps came rushing down to her side, and strong hands reached out to take hold of her.

'Are you all right?' Garde's deep voice asked.

If a hole had opened up in the sand in front of her, Lindsay would have gladly thrown herself in. She had intended to sweep out of his presence, very much on her dignity. But instead, she felt herself being lifted, bodily, and set back on her feet like a little child.

'I don't think there's any permanent damage,' he called up towards the veranda, where Eleanor's slender form was hanging anxiously over the ornate balustrade.

He thought it was funny, Lindsay was certain of it, and when she glanced up into his face, her worst fears were confirmed. The man was grinning.

'Thank you,' she forced out, doing her level best to inject a note of genuine gratitude into her voice, for Eleanor's sake if nothing else.

'No problem,' he returned, blue eyes glinting down into hers.

Moving closer, he turned her hands over in his, palms upwards, in one final, ignominious check on her person.

'I'm OK,' she insisted.

'Just let me make sure,' he persisted.

His hand rose, brushing the golden grains of sand from her tousled hair, and she couldn't move. Gently, he dusted her down, his long fingers moving lightly over her shoulders, smoothing away any lingering remnants of the beach still caught up on her person.

'That's better,' he said softly.

Luckily, Jack had spotted her, and his voice shattered the growing spell between them. He was racing across the beach, arms outflung, and abruptly, she took a step away, out of Garde's mesmerising presence. She felt him leave her side, heard his footsteps take him away, back to the veranda.

40

'Mummy, it's me.'

The child reached her at last, flinging himself at her legs in a flurry of sand, and she snatched him up, clutching him to her. Then Chrissie came running over to join them, her long hair blowing about her face.

'Hi, Lindsay, coming to play?' she called.

Of course, Lindsay was coming! She couldn't wait. Dropping Jack to the ground, they raced after Chrissie, leaving Garde and the veranda well and truly behind. Together they paddled in the surf, trying to race the waves, swinging the child high until he screamed with delight. Then they put the finishing touches to his ever-growing castle in the sand.

The girl's enthusiastic chatter about college was unstoppable, and Lindsay found herself carried along in a fervent discussion about schools and teaching.

'Even Aunt Eleanor thinks it's a suitable career,' Chrissie told her.

'And that matters?' Lindsay queried.

'Of course, it matters,' the girl sighed, pulling a comical face. 'There could be a family connection soon. Didn't you know?'

Lindsay hesitated before replying, wary of betraying an interest she didn't want Chrissie to misunderstand.

'Maybe,' she acknowledged at last, her voice carefully even. 'I think Gardener Mitchell might have mentioned something about it.'

'Oh, Uncle Garde.' The girl laughed. 'He would, wouldn't he?'

'I suppose so.'

Lindsay shrugged, her suspicions confirmed. Garde and Eleanor—that was the family connection Chrissie was talking about, wasn't it?

'Though we have to be so careful,' Chrissie went on, her face grave, a faintly tremulous smile on her young lips, 'or it might never happen. Aunt Eleanor isn't well, you know. No one is supposed to do anything to upset her, anything at all. A shock could be fatal.'

The world stopped dead in its tracks, its sounds fading away into the distance. Lindsay's throat seemed to have closed completely, and she swallowed hard. Fatal? Even accounting for youthful exaggeration, it could only mean one thing. A shock might kill Eleanor. No wonder Garde was so protective.

'Really?' she managed quietly.

'Mm,' Chrissie returned with a sigh.

So it was true. Jamie's mother was ill, very ill. The colour drained from Lindsay's face. She was shaking inside, her hands icy, her eyes confused. That dreadful Gardener Mitchell was right, after all. She'd have to watch every move she made, every word she said, if she didn't want to make matters worse.

CHAPTER THREE

With dazed grey eyes, Lindsay leaned forward, patting the sandcastle with slender, distracted hands. Poor Eleanor. It was dreadful news to take in, and what would she do about Jack?

'Mummy, you're spoiling my castle.'

His voice came from beside her, insistently calling her name, and she stopped dead, suddenly aware that she'd been systematically flattening one of its major fortifications.

'Sorry, baby,' she said gently, carefully returning the breached wall to its former sculptured glory.

'Lindsay,' Chrissie queried, 'are you OK? You look a bit pale to me.'

At once, Lindsay smiled, gently patting the girl's hand.

'Of course I'm OK,' she insisted.

'Well, I'm not,' Jack announced, pulling himself up on to his chubby, bare feet with a long suffering sigh. 'I'm just starving.'

'Then lunch it is,' Lindsay said gravely. 'We can't have you starving away in front of our eyes, can we?'

It took some time to get back, with Jack skipping and singing between them. He seemed to have forgotten how hungry he was, and nearly half an hour passed before they reached the house.

It lay silent, the veranda empty. Garde obviously wasn't there, and Eleanor must be inside. Lindsay sighed with relief. She wouldn't have to run the gauntlet of his disconcerting blue eyes.

Chrissie had hold of Jack's small hand, ready to lead him off to the nursery, and for once Lindsay let him go without a protest. The girl was laughing with him, promising him banana and honey sandwiches for lunch, but she had to have lunch with Eleanor. It was expected.

'See you soon, baby,' she called after him. 'Be good for Chrissie.'

It took several minutes for her to wash and tidy herself, then she sat down at the mirror to retouch her make-up. A rather woebegone young face stared back at her, the eyes huge in the pale features, the soft mouth perilously close to drooping. She was caught between Eleanor and Jack. But Lindsay wasn't without commonsense. Bravely, she raised her head. Why all the anxiety? All she had to do was to be nice to Eleanor and try not to upset her. That wasn't too much to ask, was it? She couldn't truly mean to take over Jack's care completely.

Her fingers were surprisingly steady as she outlined her lips with a fresh coat of colour. Already, her mind was becoming clearer, her thoughts less disjointed. A brush lay on the delicate marble table top and she picked it up, flicking it through her hair to remove the tangles before confining it again in the silky ribbon at her neck. A few minutes later she descended the stairs to join Eleanor for lunch.

It was a pleasant meal, the first of many she shared with Eleanor over the next few days. Thankfully, Garde wasn't very much in evidence. He was exceptionally busy, Chrissie said, so his presence was limited to a few flying visits, giving Lindsay time to spend with Jamie's mother without him breathing down her neck all the time.

She was pleasantly surprised at how well they got on. The question of Jack's custody thankfully never came up, and she could relax, feel at home in Eleanor's house. Even when the beach party was suggested again, and for the following day into the bargain, she managed not to panic.

'Sounds good,' she said warily, though secretly, the thought of meeting all those people for the first time, made her shy spirit positively quail.

'Garde will be coming for lunch tomorrow, to help me plan it all,' Eleanor added with a smile.

That idea was even less welcome, and Lindsay had to struggle to keep the smile on her face. But what could she say? Admitting she didn't want him there would bring about too many awkward questions, questions for which she hadn't a single ready answer.

Saying she just didn't like him was hardly a good reason, especially to the woman who loved him. Telling her something like that wouldn't exactly be taking good care of Eleanor, so Lindsay kept resolutely silent.

'How nice,' she managed to force out.

Lunch the next day was a cold collation set out on a long, polished sideboard. But it was no casual picnic meal, not under Marsha's eagle-eyed supervision. A set of silver serving dishes contained the widest choice of foods Lindsay had ever seen outside a restaurant.

She lifted one lid, then another, drawn by the mouthwatering aroma of a homemade herb and vegetable quiche. Once it had been located, she helped herself to a modest slice. Some rice salad followed, together with a spoonful of crispy mushrooms and a couple of tiny, sweet tomatoes.

Carefully, she carried her plate through to the dining table, but her eyes darted surreptitiously ahead. She just couldn't stop them. Was Gardener Mitchell already there?

Yes, she noted gloomily, he was lounging at ease in the seat opposite Eleanor, deep in conversation. But Eleanor glanced up, smiling, as Lindsay made her way towards them.

'Come and sit here,' she invited, 'where I can see you properly.'

She pointed to a chair on the other side of the table, facing her, and Lindsay found herself sitting beside the very person she wanted to avoid at all costs. Fervently, she felt herself wishing she could have eaten with Chrissie and Jack in the nursery, but no one would ever have known that.

Her face was a perfect picture of unconcern as she slid into her seat.

'We aren't usually so informal,' Eleanor continued, 'but with guests coming this afternoon, Marsha's busy in the kitchen.'

'I don't mind serving myself,' Lindsay returned evenly, lifting a forkful of quiche smoothly to her mouth, quickly followed by another.

'I like to see a healthy appetite in the young,' Garde reflected gravely.

Eleanor laughed out loud, leaning over the table to pat his lean hand.

'Don't tease,' she admonished with an amused gleam in her eyes. 'Leave poor Lindsay alone until she knows you better.'

'Do you think Lindsay wants to know me better?' Garde broke in, his tone touched with humour.

It almost killed Lindsay to smile back. For one wild moment she was tempted to throw caution to the winds and blurt out the truth. She knew him quite well enough already, thanks very much! But Eleanor was dimpling over at him, so Lindsay managed to keep her wayward tongue under control.

'Of course, I do,' she concurred at last.

'There,' Eleanor crowed triumphantly, her

eyes fixed insistently on Garde's handsome countenance, 'I told you so. Now you can take care of her at the picnic this afternoon.'

Horror seemed to freeze Lindsay's tongue to the roof of her mouth.

'But I'm not sixteen any more,' she protested. 'Honestly, I don't need looking after.'

Eleanor rose from her chair and came round to Lindsay's side of the table, her eyes very gentle.

'Oh, my dear,' she murmured, 'I know how shy you can be, meeting people you don't know, and I have to stay here in the house. But with Garde to take care of you, you needn't worry. You can enjoy yourself on the beach.'

Fat chance, Lindsay almost groaned aloud. There was nothing left to do but to give way, as graciously as she could, and accept the inevitable. Garde was going to partner her to the party, and she had to make the best of it.

'And now that's settled,' Garde said, rising from his chair with an easy grace, 'I must be going. But don't worry,' he added, bending again to drop a swift kiss on to Eleanor's smooth cheek, 'I'll be back in time to play escort to Lindsay.'

Marsha came to see him out, and as soon as his tall personage had disappeared from the room, Eleanor smiled over at her young guest.

'And how's darling Jack?' she enquired, her face alight with tenderness.

48

Apprehension caught abruptly in Lindsay's throat. They hadn't talked a lot about Jack, and she didn't want to start again now. Trust the subject to come up as soon as that awful man was about.

'He's very well, and he already loves Chrissie to bits,' she nodded, somehow finding the courage to respond.

'I thought he would,' Eleanor enthused, a note of satisfaction inserting itself into her voice. 'It was Garde's idea, you know,' she prattled on. 'I told him I wanted to get someone to help with Jack, and straightaway, he suggested Chrissie.'

Wildly, Lindsay's hackles rose. Garde? Trust it to have been him. Couldn't he ever keep his opinions to himself?

'Garde?' she demanded. 'What has Jack got to do with him?'

'Nothing, I suppose.'

A note of doubt edged into Eleanor's voice, and she glanced over at Lindsay.

'Is something wrong?' she queried.

With commendable restraint, Lindsay bit her lip. Just the look on Eleanor's pale countenance was enough to make her think again.

'Of course not,' she promised. 'Stop worrying, we're having a party today, remember? So what are you going to wear?'

It was a fortuitous change of subject, and Lindsay drew a shaky sigh of relief. It seemed

Eleanor was having some trouble deciding on her clothes for the afternoon. A choice, apparently, between a semi-fitted dress in soft russet linen or a cooler, flowered, loose dress.

'Can you see me in flowers?' she asked anxiously.

'You'll look good, whatever you choose,' Lindsay reassured her, though her bet was on the russet linen. Even at a tea party, she couldn't really imagine that impeccable Eleanor in a loose-flowing, casual smock!

Half an hour later, she left Eleanor happily occupied in her dressing-room, and she headed upstairs to look in on Jack. Her small son was fast asleep, his chubby body stretched out flat on his little blue bed. Gently, she smoothed a wayward curl from his dreaming face.

'I thought I'd let him sleep for a while,' Chrissie whispered.

Lindsay nodded and left, leaving the girl to get on with the important task of reading a pile of the latest glossy fashion magazines. Her own room was quiet, delightfully quiet, and she flopped thankfully on to the satin draped bed, her slender body relaxing into its comforting softness.

At home, it would never enter her head to take a lunchtime nap. But here, keeping Eleanor happy was sometimes a bit like walking on eggshells, and almost at once her thoughts began to drift slowly.

She woke with a start half an hour later when Jack burst into her room. He jumped straight on to the bed, landing with a thump on her chest.

'Mummy, can I wear my Mickey Mouse T-shirt?' he called out, laughing, the tip of his nose no more than an inch or so from her own.

'Oh dear,' she groaned, her hand to her throat. 'I can't breathe! You're so fat, you're squashing me to death!'

That was the signal for a wrestling match that went on until she finally pinned his wriggling little body to the quilt.

'Now I can kiss you all over,' she promised, her face quite straight, and she proceeded to do just that, from his nose to the ends of his toes.

'Stop, stop,' he begged at last, giggling helplessly.

He pulled himself free and stretched up to his full height in front of her.

'Chrissie says I have to wash for my nana's party,' he said gravely.

Chrissie again, Lindsay noted wryly, and my nana. Her son was growing up fast. Already his world was expanding beyond his mother.

'Off you go,' she laughed. 'I'll see you later, when you're all clean.'

With a satisfied nod, he flashed her a final smile and disappeared into the nursery. Lindsay rose then to her own feet. Lying full-length in her pale pink marble bath suddenly

51

seemed liked a very good idea, and within minutes, she had slipped up to her neck in warm, scented bubbles.

But the unsettling image of Garde's suntanned face rose inexorably behind her closed lids, its strong features determined to haunt her. Dear heavens, why did the man get under her skin so much? She had a whole afternoon to get through in his company.

For heaven's sake, she told herself sharply, what on earth are you worrying about? Nothing can happen in broad daylight on a beach full of Eleanor's friends.

There was going to be nothing formal about the party, Eleanor had insisted, so Lindsay wore something fairly casual. She didn't go quite as far as the minute shorts Chrissie seemed to favour so much, though her legs were long and shapely, and every bit as good to look at. Instead, she pulled a cool skirt in crisp cotton poplin over her hips. In kingfisher blue covered in a tiny daisy print, it was matched with a matching camisole top in fitted broderie anglais. Turning her attention to her hair, she left a few golden tendrils loose for once, hanging in wayward curls about her face. The rest, she drew back.

'You look lovely, my dear,' Eleanor said when Lindsay went to find her.

'You, too,' Lindsay returned.

Eleanor had chosen the russet linen. It was draped in soft, autumnal folds about her

52

slender, reclining form.

It was a lovely afternoon for an outdoor party. The sun was high in the sky, casting sharply dappled shadows on to the garden's rolling green lawns, and the sweet scent of fragrant tropical blossoms hung in the shimmering air. Maralyn Clarke, Eleanor's oldest friend, was the first guest to arrive, putting in an appearance just after three o'clock.

'Is this Lindsay?' she trilled, her eyes fixed on Lindsay's smiling countenance. 'I know I'm early,' she added, tripping across the veranda to give Eleanor an all-enveloping hug, 'but I always like to be the first, especially on a day like this, meeting your new family.'

'You always were the pushy one, even at school,' Eleanor said laughingly, returning the hug with interest.

'She's even beaten me to the door this time.'

It was Garde's deep voice, coming suddenly out of nowhere. He strode into sight, appearing like some bronzed genie at the foot of the veranda steps, looking up at them with smiling blue eyes.

'Well, now she's here,' Eleanor put in quickly, 'she can make herself useful. Come into the kitchen, Maralyn, and help me supervise Marsha.'

'Since when did Marsha need supervising?' Maralyn grumbled. 'I want to meet Jack.'

'All in good time,' Eleanor insisted, cutting

short her friend's exuberant chattering. 'He'll be down later.'

Maralyn wasn't convinced, judging by the disbelieving look on her face, but she went just the same, following Eleanor's retreating figure with a resigned shrug.

Garde watched them go, then he turned, smiling, to quirk a sardonic brow in the direction of Lindsay's silent form.

'Oh, dear,' he sighed softly. 'I think we've been left alone, to get to know each other better.'

'Possibly,' she said, trying to sound as casual as he did.

'Definitely,' he corrected smoothly. 'Wasn't that the whole idea?'

It obviously amused him to treat her like a child, and Lindsay seethed, but outwardly, she simply smiled as he came up the steps towards her.

'Anything to please Eleanor,' she agreed sweetly.

'Of course,' he concurred with a flashing smile.

Taking her arm, he escorted her to the back of the house. On the veranda, long tables covered in crisp white damask displayed a whole variety of party dainties, both savoury and sweet. But Garde made straight for one of the drinks' trolleys.

'Wine?' he enquired, and she nodded.

'Thank you,' she agreed, accepting a tall

flute of finest, chilled chablis.

They stood looking out over the beach, leaning against the carved white balustrade without speaking. Translucent and crystal clear, the blue-green waters of the bay lapped lazily along a fairytale curve of perfect white sand, while the great breakers from the ocean beyond foamed white and shimmering against the encircling reef.

It was so odd, standing there with him. He looked so relaxed for once, with that devastating smile on his face. Whether she liked it or not, she had to admit his attentions were far from unpleasant.

'Perhaps you'd like to swim later on, since it's such a lovely day,' he asked suddenly, out of the blue, and taken aback, she nodded.

She stole a glance at the tall, muscular figure lounging beside her, registering he had changed as well, discarding his jacket for a shirt in pale blue silk, short-sleeved and open at the neck, teamed with a pair of slim, stone-coloured slacks.

Garde was staring out to sea, a hand to his eyes, shading them against the heat of the sun. Thankfully, he seemed unaware of her veiled interest.

'Look,' he pointed out, indicating towards an emerald green sail bobbing across the horizon. 'It's the Leahi, the racing catamaran. She gives sunset sails from Waikiki beach to help fund the owner's races.'

'You mean, not everyone here is a millionaire?' she said, her eyes resting on the billowing green sail disappearing into the distance.

'Not quite everyone,' he replied with a grin.

Chatting to him was growing easier every minute. He was charming company, laughing and gently teasing, not treating her like a child at all, and she found herself laughing back, all shyness forgotten.

'I think I will go swimming,' she reflected aloud.

'Fine,' came his immediate response. 'I'll probably join you.'

'Oh, good.'

Something in her voice must have caught his attention, some slight hesitation. He subjected her to a minute appraisal, a smile hovering at the corners of his mouth, one quizzical brow raised.

'If that's OK with you, of course,' he enquired very softly.

'Why not?' she replied, pushing her doubts aside with an airy wave of her hand. 'As you said before, it's a wonderful day, and this must be the best view in the islands.'

'I can't argue with that,' he allowed softly.

His voice was a soft murmur, his tone warm, like dark velvet. The eyes looking her over were a deep, speculative blue. A faint betraying flush rose in Lindsay's cheeks. Garde regarded her in silence for several long moments more, his gaze locked deep into hers. They were so close, their shoulders were virtually touching. Lindsay could feel his breath warm on her cheek. Abruptly, her heart leaped into overdrive, beating like a drum under her ribs. They didn't move, didn't speak. Then, finally, at long last, Garde broke the silence between them, his voice very soft.

'Let's go and meet the guests,' he suggested.

Gratefully, she nodded, taking his arm, grateful for the excuse to get back inside.

At least twenty guests were expected that afternoon. They were Eleanor's closest friends and neighbours, and Garde introduced Lindsay to them all. Most of the names went right over her head, there were just too many to remember at one time, except for Nancy and Orrin Richards. They were tenants of one of Eleanor's pineapple plantations a few miles along the highway, and they made well and truly certain she wouldn't forget them.

Rather younger than Eleanor and with two bouncy teenage children in tow, they never seemed to stop talking. When they cornered her in the library door, Lindsay thought she'd be there for good.

'And where's little Jack?' Nancy gushed. 'Eleanor's talked so much about him. He must be the luckiest boy in the world.'

'Lucky?' Lindsay queried, her face wary.

'To inherit all this,' Orrin said with a grin. 'Say, we haven't spoiled the surprise, have we?'

he continued. 'I thought it was all settled.'

Shaken, Lindsay stared. She knew she was goggling over at them like the veritable village idiot, but she just couldn't stop herself.

'I don't know what you mean,' she finally managed to say.

Garde was at her elbow in a moment, and swiftly he whisked her away, fending off the questions with a faintly apologetic smile.

'What were they talking about?' she demanded as soon as they were safely out of earshot.

'After the party Eleanor will tell you herself,' Garde began.

'I want to know now!'

'After the party,' he insisted. 'Now, we really must circulate.'

He'd made up his mind. She could see it in his face. Politely, but firmly, he guided her towards the latest arrival, and gritting her teeth in exasperation, Lindsay had no choice but to go.

'This is Jeffrey Perlman,' Garde introduced with one of his smoothest smiles. 'He's one of my firm's junior associates.'

'Call me Jeff,' the young man invited. 'Everyone else does.'

It was a nice name, Jeff. Nice and normal, without any complicated hidden depths. His smile was nice, too, and she smiled back.

'Thank you, Jeff,' she responded, taking his outstretched hand.

His clasp was warm, firm without being pushy, like he seemed himself, and she smiled again, sure she was going to like him.

'Chrissie is outside,' Garde broke in, indicating towards the beach. 'I think she's expecting you.'

'Thank you, Mr Mitchell, sir.'

Jeff shot him a grateful smile, but he was already halfway across the floor, making his way towards the open door.

'He's my niece's latest conquest,' Garde explained.

'Good for her,' she replied.

Outside it was very hot, and from the veranda they could see the wide, bright beach stretched out in front of them. A couple of heads bobbed lazily up and down in the tranquil waters, while a few brave souls were sunning themselves on the open sands.

One of the Richards' boys, the youngest one with the crewcut, called her name, his young voice ringing out above the rhythmic surge of the waves, and she raised a hand to acknowledge him.

By the steps lay a neatly-folded pile of towels, thoughtfully provided by Eleanor for her guests, and Garde collected a couple. He walked her down on to the sands, a hand lightly at her elbow.

'This will do,' she insisted, stopping dead before they'd gone too far, and pointing to a shady spot under a nearby group of palms.

It wasn't too far from Jack. She could see him hopping about by Chrissie and Jeff, a cake in one small hand, a peach in another, so it suited her admirably. She wanted him where she could see him.

'As you wish,' Garde said, nodding his agreement, and he dropped the towels to the ground.

He stripped off his shirt, pulling it over his head without a second's hesitation, and her eyes widened as it floated down like a blue silk butterfly on to the golden sand. His naked chest hovered above her, broad and bronzed and covered by a faint mist of fine hair as dark as the hair on his head. Hastily, she averted her gaze, letting it fix on a spot just in front of his left foot. But that was bare, too, as he kicked off his shoes. Heavens above, had the man no modesty in him?

'Coming to swim?' he enquired, and at her continued silence, he added with a hint of laughter in his tone, 'You don't mind if I go, do you?'

Mind? She could scarcely wait to be rid of him, but she could hardly tell him that to his feet. It would look too odd for words. So she dared a brief glance upwards. Wearing nothing but a pair of denim swimshorts, Garde towered above her, looking larger than ever with no clothes to disguise the strength of his powerful frame.

'Not at all,' she conceded in a small voice.

'I won't go far,' he promised.

'Please yourself,' she replied, attempting nonchalance.

He could go as far as he liked. She wouldn't be following. His presence was often charming, usually interesting, but always, always, disturbing. She was constantly on edge, and all the time trying to appear as cool as a cucumber. She was heartily glad of the chance to relax.

As soon as Garde had gone, she slipped off her dress to reveal a brief scarlet swimsuit beneath. Even there, under the trees, it was still very hot, and in a matter of seconds, she spread out her towel on the hot sand and stretched herself full-length on its soft surface.

With a sigh, Lindsay closed her eyes. Peace at last. But she should have known it wouldn't last. She half-opened one eye as a child's laughing voice breathed into her ear, and her son's small body came snuggling up to her.

'Can I lie here with you?' he demanded, planting a huge, beachy kiss on her mouth.

'I'd love it,' she replied.

It was true. She did. He was the one person in the world she was always happy to see, and she hugged him tight. His skin was still as soft as a baby's, and she relished the gorgeous feel of his wriggling little body against hers.

'Luv you,' he said, treating her to another sloppy kiss.

'Me, too,' she insisted.

But if she was harbouring any vague hope he'd lie quietly and sunbathe, she was sadly mistaken. He lined up row upon row of tiny shells for her to admire, a feat which kept him occupied for fully ten minutes.

'What shall we do now?' he enquired. 'I know, we'll go swimming,' he sang out.

Going down to the sea wasn't part of her plans. Garde was down there, and he wasn't part of her plans, either. She needed some peace from him, time apart from his disturbing presence. She didn't know what to think about him any more. Her feelings were confused, uncertain, and she'd never get the chance to sort them out, not with him about all the time.

'But what about your shells?' she prevaricated.

'No more,' Jack insisted, shaking his head, and as if to make sure, he ran a hand through the ordered rows, mixing the shells up in the sand.

There was nothing else she could do to distract him, and Lindsay shrugged, knowing she was defeated. Resigned, she took her son's hand.

'To the sea,' she said finally.

CHAPTER FOUR

'Where's Garde?' Jack demanded, glancing all around as they reached the frothing water's edge.

Lindsay put her hand up to shade her eyes, pretending she couldn't find him, but her son's gaze soon saw out the suntanned figure in the distance.

'Come on, Mummy,' he said, impatiently tugging her hand.

They began to splash along the edge of the waves, making their way towards the man swimming effortlessly in the surf.

'Hi,' he called out, waving towards them.

'Jack was wondering where you were,' Lindsay informed him, not wanting him to think the interest might come from her.

She pushed the child forward, and without a word he lifted the boy high on his shoulders. Jack was laughing with delight, being so high above the world, and Lindsay had to smile herself. Garde was towering above her, drops of crystal clear water glistening all over his sunbronzed frame, with Jack's grinning face above his dark head.

Somehow, the idea of splashing them both insinuated itself into her mind, and she didn't attempt to fight it, scooping handfuls of water in their direction until the pair of them were soaked from head to foot.

'Lindsay,' Garde shouted, trying vainly to save himself while hanging grimly on to Jack.

'Don't be a spoilsport,' she accused, 'Jack loves the water,' and she flung another drenching armful towards them, laughing aloud.

Garde didn't take the onslaught again without protest. With one sharp glance in her direction, he dropped Jack gently at her feet.

'We think you should join in as well,' he said softly.

He scooped her up as if she weighed no more than the proverbial feather, high into his arms, carrying her without the slightest effort.

'Garde,' she protested, 'that's enough. Put me down at once.'

'Whatever you say,' he agreed softly, and he dropped her into the sea.

Lindsay hadn't expected him to obey quite so soon, and placid or not, it came as quite a shock when the warm sea water closed over her head. She surfaced again to the roaring surge of the waves. She just had time to catch a glimpse of Jack, round-eyed and staring, before Garde's strong hands reached out once more, setting her firmly back on her own two feet.

'Don't worry, you're quite safe,' he said, grinning down at her, quite openly, as if he was really enjoying himself.

The sea was softly hissing about them as

they stood in the surf, and she could feel its salty wetness over her creamy skin. Garde's skin was wet, too, but she didn't move away, not at once. She was far too breathless.

'Are you all right?' he asked.

His voice seemed very far away, echoing from somewhere across the far side of the universe. Wordlessly, she nodded. Finally, she managed a step or two away from him, but the day was so bright, the sea so sparkling and fresh, she started to run, her hair blowing about in the breeze. She snatched Jack up, whirling him high against the luminous sky.

It was amazing how well Jack took to Garde, and Garde had endless patience. Between them, they swung Jack high, holding his hands as he rose higher and higher, then they found a rock pool to explore.

'See the shells,' Garde pointed out to the intent little face.

'Mm,' the boy whispered.

They watched until it was getting too dark to see. The sun was dropping towards the horizon, and at a guess, there wasn't an hour of daylight left. One swift glance confirmed they were the only people left on the beach.

'I'll carry him back,' Garde offered quietly, and without waiting for an answer he lifted Jack high on his shoulders.

Lindsay didn't protest. Jack was getting tired, and besides, the boy obviously liked being with Garde. Men weren't usually so

65

available in his small world.

'Race you, Mummy,' he called as Garde began to stride away.

Garde didn't leave her, though. To Jack's childish dismay, he turned back towards her, holding out a hand, and it closed over hers, immeasurably warm and strong.

'We won't win now,' the little boy stated glumly.

'But we can't leave Mummy by herself,' Garde replied. 'Not out here on the beach when it's getting dark.'

'No,' Jack said slowly.

He didn't sound terribly convinced, Lindsay noted wryly. Evidently, Garde was another of the people he'd taken into his world—Chrissie, Nana, and now Garde. Her lovely son really was growing up.

'And Nana has something to tell us,' Garde continued, the words intruding into her reverie.

At once, Lindsay drew in a sharp, convulsive breath. Eleanor's announcement about Jack—how could it have slipped her mind? Collecting her towel in silence, she gave Jack a hasty rub before wrapping it round herself. Once she was dry, she slipped her dress over her head and followed her son's small figure on to the veranda. Garde had pulled on his shirt and trousers and he ushered them both inside.

The corridor stretched out before her, seeming longer than Lindsay ever remembered

66

before, and by the time they reached the sitting-room door, she could hardly breathe. Eleanor was half-reclining on her sofa bed, a shawl wrapped carefully about her narrow shoulders, and she looked up as they came into the room.

'Lindsay,' she called, putting out her hands.

Lindsay's heart contracted sharply, noting with painful concern the pale fragility of those smiling features.

'We're right here,' she responded softly.

'And where's my Jack?' Eleanor queried, her voice taking on a teasing note.

The boy ran forward, climbing with a chuckle on to his grandmother's knee. Quickly, Lindsay went to her side, taking a seat on the sofa bed, and Garde was right behind. Crossing the room in swift strides, he bent to brush his lips against the parchment-pale curve of Eleanor's temple.

'Don't tire yourself out,' he chided gently.

'You worry too much about me,' she returned with mock severity, but with such a degree of affection in her tone that Lindsay's blood chilled.

She lifted a hand, and with trembling fingers she brushed a few wayward strands of hair from her face, trying to understand the dull feeling of emptiness filling her heart. It wasn't possible. She couldn't be feeling this loss, this sudden pain, not over Garde. He was a friend, a companion, nothing more. Anything else was simply unthinkable. Carefully, she composed her features as she turned towards Eleanor.

'So,' she queried with a smile, 'what is this big secret?'

Eleanor didn't answer at once, but her eyes positively glowed.

'It's about Jack,' she sighed. 'I'm making arrangements to adopt him officially as my heir.'

There was a pleased murmur of assent in the room, a lot of smiles and congratulations, but Lindsay's throat closed painfully. These were the very words she hadn't wanted to hear.

'Adopt Jack?' she asked softly. 'What does that mean?'

'It means he becomes part of Eleanor's family,' Garde stated smoothly.

'But he's Jamie's son,' Lindsay said. 'He's already part of the family.'

'I just want to make things official, my dear. Jack wasn't born here. He needs to take American citizenship, just to make sure.'

Make sure of what? Lindsay turned at the sound of Eleanor's voice, her eyes dull, disbelieving. For what seemed an age, she didn't move, trying to think of something to say. This was Eleanor, Jamie's mother. How could she cause her any more pain? Jamie would never want that.

'I don't know,' she managed at last, her eyes darkening as she struggled with her wish to protect Eleanor and the heartstopping fear she might lose her son.

Then Jeff Perlman came to stand beside her, a look of concern invading his young face.

'Lindsay,' he said slowly, 'is this what you want?'

'Of course it's what she wants,' Garde put in at once, moving quickly to stand between them. 'She knew all about it before she came here.'

Not strictly true, but he was being the perfect lawyer again, cool, collected, protecting Eleanor's interests. But enough was enough! Lindsay had her own interests to consider as well, and she couldn't just toss them away. Jamie wouldn't want that, either.

'As I told you in London,' she reminded him quickly, 'all I've ever wanted for Jack is a family of his own.'

'Well, he certainly has that now,' Garde said with an easy smile.

She nodded, slowly, throwing him a reflective look from beneath her lowered lashes. She had to be careful, very careful, if she was going to emerge from this tangle in one piece and still keep her son.

'True,' she allowed, 'but we're spoiling the party with all this talk. Eleanor's made her announcement. That's all that matters now. We can discuss the details another time.'

She disentangled Jack's chubby body from Eleanor's arms, and she lifted him close. He was hers. He would always be hers.

'You're tired, let Chrissie take him,' Eleanor began, but Lindsay shook her head.

'No,' she said firmly. 'No, Eleanor. I want to put him to bed myself.'

She smiled, hoping to take some of the sting out of the words. But she had to be firm. Eleanor had everyone on her side, Garde on her side. She had only herself to rely on.

'I'm sure Chrissie won't mind,' Garde broke in, his tone dry.

His eyes rested indulgently on the slim figure of his niece as she edged closer to Jeff, and Chrissie laughed. She took Jeff's outstretched hand, her eyes holding an answering twinkle.

'I'll manage,' she dimpled, throwing Garde a slanting look.

Swiftly, Lindsay got to her feet, but if she hoped to slide from the room without any more comment, she had reckoned without Garde.

'Good-night, Lindsay,' he called, drawing all eyes to her departing figure again. 'We'll talk in the morning.'

The words couldn't have sounded more casual, more friendly, but somehow, they sent a shiver of dread running along Lindsay's spine. Did he mean about Jack, or the adoption? She turned to look at him, fighting to keep a polite smile on her face.

'I'll look forward to it,' she answered.

The coolness in her voice surprised her. She

didn't feel cool. But her head was high, her grey eyes calm. Forcing herself to move naturally, she carried her son across the room. No one would ever have guessed the emotions churning inside her, not beneath that serene, smiling exterior.

'I'll be here first thing,' he promised.

'I'll be waiting,' she nodded back.

Mercifully, her hand finally found the door handle before he could say any more, and she turned it quickly. She couldn't wait to get away. The need to be alone was suddenly overwhelming.

She took the stairs at a positive run, even with Jack asleep on her shoulder, and she reached her bedroom door with an overwhelming sense of relief. The boy stirred in his sleep but he didn't wake, and Lindsay stripped off his clothes as swiftly as she could.

He rolled on to his tummy the second she settled him down. Completely relaxed, he lay with one small hand outflung, the other tucked under his cheek. He looked so peaceful, a wry smile tugged at Lindsay's lips. Bless his heart, he wasn't plagued by doubts, wondering whom he could trust in this new world of theirs. If only her own life was so easy.

Lindsay sat in silence, watching his gentle breathing, until her own tired lids began to droop. Then, with a sigh, she went into her own room, leaving him to sleep. Beyond her window, darkness had fallen in a glorious sunset of crimson and gold, but Lindsay slipped beneath the covers without sparing it a second glance, far too tired to take notice. She fell asleep almost at once, but she woke again in the small hours with a sudden, violent start.

Hastily, she sat up, her heart thumping, straining to hear what had startled her. But there wasn't a sound in the house. The silence was deep, all-encompassing, and Lindsay made herself lie down again.

There's nothing wrong, she tried to tell herself. But somehow, the words weren't any comfort. For what seemed like an age, she stared at the ceiling, blindly waiting for sleep to claim her again, but it was hopeless.

Perhaps a drink might help, she mused. The night was hot, and a glass of iced fruit juice would certainly go down well. Slipping out of bed, she went to check on Jack. He was still sleeping peacefully when she glanced in, his curly head nestled into the pillows, so she made her way to the stairs.

When she reached the kitchen, there was a full moon shining in through the windows, illuminating the room with a silvery glow, enough for her to find the fridge without any need to flick on the light. There was a tumbler on the tiled worktop, and she filled it from a carton of fresh orange juice. Maybe, if she took it back to her room, she would finally go back to sleep.

Pausing in front of the window, she lifted a

hand, pressing the cold glass of the tumbler against her flushed cheek. Her mind drifted, filled with a host of images, not least of Garde, the incredible man who had taken her under his wing for the day. Eleanor had been right, she sighed. She had enjoyed his company at the party, maybe, more than enjoyed it?

No! She would never believe that. A painful throbbing began behind her temple, and she closed her eyes. She would always love Jamie. Quickly, she tried to conjure up his face, bring his lost features into her mind, but they were misty, indistinct. All she could see clearly was Garde. She winced, pushing the image firmly away. Garde wasn't for her. He never would be for her. Didn't he belong to Jamie's mother?

Confused, overtired, and consumed with doubts, she carried her glass to the door, ready to go back to bed. But the light snapped on without any warning, and the man himself was standing facing her in the doorway. He regarded her silently for several moments.

'Well, well, Lindsay, what a surprise,' he breathed. 'I didn't know you were here. Shall I switch off the light again?'

Unable to utter a single word that made any sense, Lindsay could only dumbly shake her head. The last thing on earth she needed now was to share the darkness with Gardener Mitchell, a half-dressed Gardener Mitchell at that. She was in no fit state to cope.

'Something woke me,' she managed at last,

trying to force a modicum of normality into the situation, 'so I came down for a drink.'

'Good idea,' he broke in smoothly. 'Do you mind if I join you?'

He sounded amused. There was no doubt at all he was quite at his ease. He went to the fridge, helping himself to a can of chilled beer, his long body wrapped in nothing but a white towelling robe. A dreadful suspicion suddenly assailed her—was he spending the night with Eleanor?

Instinctively, she looked away, her face flushed, downcast, trying to pretend she hadn't guessed.

'I think I'll go now,' she stammered.

'So soon?' he queried, and he threw her a slanting glance, a tinge of amusement edging into his voice. 'You're surely not afraid of me.'

Quickly, she raised her head, meeting his eyes.

'Don't be ridiculous,' she shrugged.

She made to move past him, only to be caught by surprise as he pulled her suddenly into his arms. The strangest expression had invaded his handsome features. Sliding his hands into the small of her back, he pulled her towards him, his arms clasping her close against his powerful body.

Her eyes flew to his, searching their smoky depths. Their intent was clear, he was going to kiss her, but when he bent his head, his mouth brushing hers, she found she could only respond. His lips descended, claiming her own with a sweetness that drove every lucid thought from her mind.

Instinctively, Lindsay's young body tensed, resisting his touch, but she'd never been kissed like this before, so firmly, so tenderly. At last, the kiss ended and, with dazed eyes, her face paper white, she gazed upwards. Brooding eyes looked down into hers, deeply blue and hypnotic.

'I've wanted to do that all day,' he breathed softly.

'No,' she began and put a hand to his lips, trying to stop the words.

'But why?'

'Eleanor,' she managed to say at last, her breath coming in short, despairing gasps.

Quickly, he captured her hands, enfolding them easily in one of his own.

'This isn't about Eleanor,' he whispered. 'It's about us.'

Hopelessly, Lindsay shook her head. The tears were very close. They couldn't brush Eleanor out of the picture, pretending she didn't exist.

'Please, don't cry,' he murmured.

'Garde,' she gasped, and wildly she turned in his arms.

He let her go at once, and she took a step away, but still she couldn't escape. Garde stood like a rock between her and the door.

'There's no need to be frightened,' he

assured her but dumbly she shook her head.

She wasn't so sure about that. The feelings springing up between them almost terrified the life out of her. Slowly, he raised his hand, touching her cheek with a long, enquiring finger.

'Oh, my sweet,' he insisted, his voice soft, 'don't deny it. I know you feel the same way. I felt it all afternoon.'

'No! No!' she broke in at once, stubbornly shaking her head.

Tears threatened again. This couldn't be. She had to make him understand.

'Tell me,' he persisted, and she took a convulsive, ragged breath.

'I don't know what you mean,' she managed at last, though deep inside, she knew perfectly well what he meant.

'I don't believe you,' he said.

Stubbornly, she closed her eyes, and stood perfectly still. But his mouth descended again, sweetly, heartbreakingly soft, to gently find hers.

'Tell me,' he repeated softly. 'Tell me you don't care. Tell me now, while I'm holding you here in my arms.'

She couldn't, of course, but wordlessly, she managed to shake her head. For a moment he watched her closely, his eyes searching her delicate features, his gaze dark and inscrutable.

'Don't try to play games with me,' he

76

warned. 'You could overdo it, my sweet.'

His tone was light, but a soft thread of anger underlying the words drove the blood from Lindsay's face. But the sudden, unbidden picture of Eleanor's smiling face flashed briefly into her mind, and she swallowed convulsively. How dare he tell her not to play games.

'I really have no idea what you mean,' she repeated.

Carefully, she finished her drink and, replacing the glass on the worktop, she turned her back on him and walked unsmiling from the room.

Once in her bedroom, she lay on top of the bed, her eyes glistening with the sheen of unshed tears. Like a fool, she had let the magic of the day get under her skin. Garde had kissed her. Even worse, she had wanted him to. Well, she decided ferociously, it will never happen again.

She rolled over, her eyes fixed on the window, on the glorious wash of blues and golds heralding a brand new day. In the next room, Jack started to stir. Drearily, Lindsay got to her feet. It was time to get up.

As usual, it took a while to get her young son ready for breakfast. He was spilling over with an abundance of childish energy, and by the time he was ready, Lindsay's gloomy mood had started to lift. He was just too lively to let her stay depressed for long. She finally caught him in a vice-like grip, clean and scrubbed and bright-eyed with mischief, and began to carry him downstairs.

'Where's Chrissie?' he asked, suddenly noticing her absence.

Lindsay shook her head, a rueful smile curving her lips. The girl was probably still sleeping in after the party. No doubt, she would roll up later, apologising profusely for her absence. Good luck to her, she shrugged. Let her enjoy life while she's young. At least it gives me Jack to myself for a while. Surprisingly, Eleanor was absent, too. The dining-room was quite empty when they went in, and the table was set for only two.

'I hope you don't mind,' Marsha explained, appearing out of nowhere with the coffee, 'but madam is tired after the party, and she's resting.'

Lindsay's heart gave an uncomfortable little lurch in her chest.

'Is she all right?' she asked at once.

'Just resting,' Marsha insisted. 'Perhaps you'd like to go in after breakfast.'

'Shall I go now?'

'No,' Marsha broke in. 'Let her rest. Eat your breakfast. She's expecting you later.'

The woman's voice was light but firm, and Lindsay sank obediently into her allotted place. If Eleanor was expecting her after breakfast, then after breakfast it would be.

Marsha served the food, nothing ruffling

78

that calm exterior.

Turning to the housekeeper, Lindsay said gently, 'We can manage, Marsha. Why don't you go and see how Eleanor is?'

'You're sure?' Marsha queried. 'Madam did tell me to take care of you.'

'We can manage,' Lindsay repeated firmly.

The housekeeper nodded, taking herself out of the room without any further attempt at protest, and once she was left alone, Lindsay soon had breakfast finished. With Marsha out of the way, she didn't need to pretend any more, and she pushed her half-empty plate away in relief. It was turning her stomach!

A thought suddenly struck her, an unwelcome thought that made her cheeks disconcertingly warm. Maybe Garde would be there, in Eleanor's room when she went in.

'Mummy, you've gone all red,' her son pointed out.

'It's hot,' she explained quickly.

She insisted he had a glass of milk as well as his juice, and since Chrissie still hadn't turned up when he'd finally finished, he would have to come in with her to see Eleanor. Since she didn't want him leaving his sticky fingermarks all over his grandmother's immaculate room, she dragged him protesting to have another wash. Then with his wriggling, freshly-scrubbed hand clasped in a grip of iron, she finally knocked on Eleanor's door.

Please, she pleaded, biting her lip in silent

anguish, don't let Garde answer. She didn't think she could keep the shock from showing on her face if he did. But it was Eleanor's soft voice which invited her in and she was quite alone. There wasn't a sign of male habitation anywhere in the room, recent or otherwise, and Lindsay drew in a great, ragged sigh of relief. Eleanor was relaxing among the pillows, a tray by her side, but she lifted her hands in welcome as soon as they came in.

'My dear, how lovely to see you, and Jack as well. Sit here, won't you?'

She patted the bed, smiling up at Lindsay's still hesitant figure, but her eyes were soon back with Jack. With a wriggle, he escaped from his mother's clutches and made a running leap to his grandmother's side.

'Be careful,' Lindsay warned, but Eleanor shook her head.

'Let him be,' she said with an indulgent smile. 'I love to have him around. Sit down, my dear, and don't worry so much. You look a bit ruffled.'

'Mummy's hot,' Jack explained at once.

Maddeningly, the colour rose in Lindsay's cheeks all over again. There was no earthly way she could stop it, and she shook her head, raising her hands helplessly into the air. What could she say to that? She could hardly tell Eleanor she'd been half-expecting to see Garde's tall figure in the room.

'Anyone would be hot,' she managed at last,

'if they had to deal with a small Jack Holland first thing in the morning!'

They all laughed, and thankfully, the moment passed. They spent another half-hour chatting, but there was no mention of any plans for Jack, plans for any adoption. Lindsay had just decided to broach the subject herself when Marsha knocked, coming in to urge them out of the room.

'The doctor's here,' she announced.

'Just a routine visit,' Eleanor put in quickly, meeting Lindsay's concerned eyes. 'People are so fussy,' she said, as Marsha tutted and plumped up the pillows behind her. 'I'm afraid I'll have to rest for today, just to keep them all happy,' she added brightly. 'But don't worry. Garde will be here soon, to take you both into Waikiki.'

CHAPTER FIVE

Lindsay felt her stomach flutter in trepidation. Eleanor couldn't have said what she thought she'd said. Go into Waikiki with Garde? It just wasn't an option.

'You knew he was coming, didn't you, dear?' Eleanor queried. 'I'm sure he said so yesterday,' and when Lindsay nodded, wide-eyed with shock, she gave a satisfied smile. 'I thought so,' she sighed. 'I've asked him to look after you for today, while I'm out of action.'

'But . . . but . . .' Lindsay stammered.

She couldn't go into Waikiki with Garde. She couldn't go anywhere with Garde. After last night, she didn't trust him an inch. She didn't know if she trusted herself. They were best kept apart. Valiantly, she opened her mouth to protest. She could say she was tired after the party, and that Jack needed to rest as well. But Marsha was watching over Eleanor like a hawk.

'Enough for now,' she insisted, and she hustled them from the room.

'Bring Jack in to see me when you come back,' Eleanor called, just as the door was closed, shutting her firmly from Lindsay's sight.

Left alone in the corridor, Lindsay stood stock still. What on earth was Eleanor up to?

First the party, and now Waikiki. It didn't make sense, throwing her into Garde's company all the time. Or did it? Abruptly, her mind stilled, focusing in on one cold, clear thought. Could it be possible that if Eleanor wanted something as badly as she surely wanted Jack, might she ask Garde to help her to get it? Was that why Eleanor kept pushing Garde into her presence? Was it all part of a plan to adopt Jack?

Lindsay lifted her son into her arms, ignoring his protests, his insistence he wanted to walk, and with trembling steps, she made for the staircase. Surely, it couldn't be true. Eleanor might be rich, spoiled even, but selfish to that extent? Lindsay couldn't believe it, not of Jamie's mother. Perhaps it was all Garde's idea.

Somehow, that thought was just as bad. Shaken, she hurried Jack into the nursery, setting him down to play with his toys. Perhaps she should go with Garde, after all. That way, she might find out what was going on.

'Mummy, look.'

Jack held up a small red truck for her to admire.

'It's lovely, darling,' she agreed. 'Shall we put it in the garage?'

'But I thought you were coming out with me,' a deep voice broke in, and Lindsay glanced up to see Garde smiling across from the doorway.

She swallowed hard, but quickly she found her voice. With what she hoped was a suitable display of lightness, she smiled back.

'So Eleanor says,' she replied.

'And we must please Eleanor, mustn't we?'

'So you've always said.'

There was just the faintest edge of acid in her tone, but if he heard it, he didn't comment.

'I'll wait in the hall,' was all he said.

Lindsay nodded, absently, outwardly too busy flicking a comb through Jack's wayward locks to pay him some attention. But she'd made up her mind. She would go to Waikiki. She had to find out what was going on.

It was nine on the dot when she presented herself in the silent hall. Garde was there, waiting for them, but his face was a picture when he caught sight of the slender figure advancing towards him. His eyebrows shot up, as if he couldn't believe his eyes.

'Have you decided to travel incognito?' he enquired incredulously, noting her dark glasses and the wide-brimmed straw hat on her head.

'I was worried about the sun,' she pointed out carefully.

His eyes took in her light summer smock in deep rose pink, its fluid lines concealing all signs of her figure, the elbow-length sleeves carefully covering her slim shoulders.

'Ah, yes,' he said, 'you must protect yourself from the sun at all costs.'

'Shall we go now?' she enquired crisply.

In dignified silence, she followed him out to the car, Jack's hand clasped firmly in her own until he was safely strapped in his car seat. Then she slid into the front passenger seat. Garde closed her door, and went round to his own side of the car. Without a word, he fired the engine and the vehicle pulled away.

'I thought this was going to be a more formal occasion,' Lindsay began, referring back to their conversation of the evening before, their conversation about Jack.

'Not today,' he returned easily. 'Business can wait. This is your first visit to Waikiki. It should be happy and relaxed.'

'And a business trip won't be?' she enquired pointedly.'

He chose not to reply, and Lindsay turned to stare out of the window. Already, she had the distinct feeling it was going to be quite a day.

The mere suggestion of a breeze fanned in through the car's open window, blowing tendrils of silken hair across her face, and she was just about to close her eyes in the sunshine when Garde slowed the car almost to a halt.

'We can't miss Pine Grove Village,' he said, indicating to the side of the road. 'Let's go over and take a look. Jack might see something he likes.'

Without waiting for a reply, he manoeuvred the car across the road and parked it under the shade of several tall pine trees. He lifted Jack out, taking his small hand in his, and Lindsay had no choice but to follow.

Pine Grove turned out to be a cluster of thatched stalls laid out in the shade of a group of pines, each stall displaying a spread of colourful island wares. Smiling Polynesian women in brightly-coloured muu-muus sat beside them, nodding quiet greetings as Garde led them from stall to stall.

It was fascinating, and Lindsay wandered from stall to stall, admiring a shell here and a piece of jewellery there, until she was finally drawn to one stall in particular. It was standing a little away from the rest and she paused in front of it, admiring the array of coral necklaces on display.

'May I see that?' she breathed, her eyes bright, pointing to a sarong hanging near the back of the stall.

She couldn't resist it. The garment was in several shades of blue and green, one colour merging into the other like shot silk, and she held it up to the light. It hung between her fingers as delicate as a spider's web.

'Let me see,' Garde said, and before she could say a word, he took the garment and held it against her fair skin. 'It could have been made for you,' he added, his eyes resting musingly on the smooth, creamy oval of her face.

'I'm glad you like it,' Lindsay managed,

shrugging, her voice carefully even.

She tried to tell herself she couldn't care less about his admiration and his smooth compliments. But she wasn't at all sure if she really meant it.

'It is beautiful,' the stallholder said. 'Right for a young woman in love.'

Caught off-guard, Lindsay could only stare. The woman obviously thought she and Garde were a couple, and she felt her body quiver slightly. For a moment, the briefest moment, Garde's eyes held hers, his gaze infinitely speculative. Then he handed the shimmering garment back to the little stallholder, and the moment was gone.

'We'll take it,' he stated softly, as Lindsay gritted her teeth, bending to busy herself with Jack.

She didn't want the sarong as a gift from him. It was too personal. It meant too much. But courtesy prevented her from telling him that in public.

'Thank you,' she murmured politely, and as she straightened up, ready to leave, the Hawaiian stallholder took a necklace of tiny, white shells from the display and placed it gently round her slender neck.

'For you,' she said, 'a present to say aloha.'

Jack was delighted. His small fingers touched the string of shells in wide-eyed wonder, and he laughed up at Garde.

'Look,' he grinned, 'my mummy's a

Hawaiian lady now.'

They went back to the car and climbed in, but Lindsay couldn't bring herself to indulge in any more small talk.

With a crunch of tyres, they pulled away. She sat still and stared sightlessly out of the window. Soon, they were driving into Waikiki. It couldn't have been more different from Eleanor's countryside home, its shops full, the streets packed with chattering people, but Garde had no difficulty in parking the car. Lindsay sat quietly as he slid the huge vehicle into a private parking garage.

'I didn't realise Waikiki was so big,' she ventured at last.

'It's not much different from any big city,' he returned evenly.

'Except for the palm trees,' she said laughingly.

'And the sunshine, and the beach,' he agreed with a grin.

Escorting them carefully through the crowds, he kept a firm grip on Jack's small hand when they crossed the busy roads.

'I think we'll see King's Alley first,' he said, pointing with a smile to a wide, sunny square.

Jack was delighted by the cobbled streets and quaint bowfronted shops, not to mention the red-coated soldiers standing on guard.

'It's modelled on Victorian England,' Garde told him.

'Can we see them march?' the little boy

queried.

'Another day, maybe,' Lindsay told him.

They paused at a lei stall to buy Jack a grasshopper woven from palm leaves. The little toy was meant to signify good luck, and Garde folded it carefully into the child's hand.

'Now you'll live in Hawaii for ever,' Garde told him softly, and Lindsay's eyes narrowed.

Not unless I have some say in the matter, she vowed.

The stall was cool and dim, a welcome oasis in all the heat and bustle, and Lindsay was in no hurry to move away. It was lovely just to stand there, surrounded by blossoms, every breath she took filling her head with their sweet perfume.

'They're so beautiful,' she said.

'Then you must have one,' Garde said and he lifted down one of the garlands of frangipani, and before she could move, he slipped it around her neck, the delicate sweetness of its fragrance overwhelming.

'Thank you,' she murmured.

'You're welcome,' he answered back.

The strangest feeling took hold of her, like being cast adrift on an unknown sea, and disconcerted, Lindsay moved a step away, clutching Jack by the hand.

'Can we see the beach?' she enquired quickly. 'I can't come to Waikiki and not see Waikiki Beach.'

'Absolutely,' Garde agreed.

He ushered them back through the busy streets, and within a few minutes they were out on the beach itself. The surf was surging in along the world-famous sands, and the great green mass of Diamond Head reared high against a brilliant blue horizon.

'Look,' she said, pointing towards an elegant shape bobbing gently in the swell of the waves.

She had to shade her eyes to see it properly, a catamaran silhouetted against the sun, its curving green sail fretting in the light sea breeze.

'It's the Leahi,' Garde reminded her softly. 'Remember? She makes trips around Diamond Head.'

'Come on,' she urged, 'let's go. I've never been on a catamaran before.'

For a moment Garde hesitated, as if he was going to refuse, then he sighed, shaking his head.

'Why can I never resist a pretty woman?' he said in mock despair.

The Leahi was dancing on the end of her restraining rope, as if she was eager to be off, and friendly hands reached out to help them up. Once on board, though, Lindsay began to wonder if she'd done the right thing. The deck was lifting and falling under her feet, quite markedly. At once, Garde sensed her uncertainty, and sliding an arm about her waist, he guided her firmly into a seat. Then the catamaran moved slowly away from the shore.

The vessel flew like an arrow over the waves. Breathlessly, Lindsay sank back into the strong circle of Garde's arm, and he scooped her to him, holding her securely against the powerful rise and fall of the yacht. It was so easy to sink against him, rocked by the wind and the sea, allowing her head to rest gently against his broad shoulder.

'Look,' he said into her ear, pointing towards the distant shore.

She gazed obediently across the rolling Pacific, to the Waikiki skyline silhouetted clearly against the horizon. The beach of deep gold was backed by an impressive sweep of luxury high-rise hotels. From where they were sitting, they could clearly see the crater of Diamond Head rearing high above the coastline at Kahala. Garde turned Jack's small face towards the magnificent sight.

'See inside the volcano,' he whispered.

'Can you go right in?' the boy queried.

'Oh, yes.' Garde smiled back. 'I'll take you one day.'

Lindsay sighed, her mind full of the shifting waves and the sound of wind against canvas. The speed of the catamaran had whipped roses into her cheeks and a diamond brightness into her eyes, and tendrils of golden hair curled damply about her face.

'That was pure magic,' she breathed as they

headed again for the shore.

On slightly shaky legs, she allowed Garde to help her through the shallows. The sand felt very firm and hard under her bare feet as they waded the last few yards.

'Come on, Jack,' she whispered. 'We'll have a burger for lunch.'

The burger bar was full to bursting, so Garde insisted on collecting the food for them all. Lindsay had to hide a smile at the sight of the usually oh-so-correct lawyer trying to balance a tray loaded with milk shakes and giant hamburgers. But she managed to get the grin off her face before he came back to the table.

Jack was in his element, sucking away at his straw. But Garde was having some difficulty with his milkshake. Lindsay had to show him how to poke the straw in through the container lid.

'You mean, you drink through that?' he exclaimed.

'You drink through that,' she affirmed dryly.

He managed to get the hang of it at last, but not without a great deal of smothered laughter on both their parts. But he attacked his hamburger with far more aplomb.

'I'm not just a pretty face,' he grinned, and Lindsay's gaze rose skywards.

'And modesty is obviously your middle name,' she remarked, but before she could think of any better way of cutting him down to size, Jack caught hold of her arm.

Holding his breath, the little boy held out his hand, and a single sparrow flew down from the trees. It was evidently a little braver than its fellows, perching on Jack's outstretched finger for a split second to snatch the morsel of bread he was holding out.

'Did you see that?' Lindsay gasped.

'Waikiki is special,' Garde confided softly. 'Even the birds are magic.'

Lindsay attempted a smile, but it failed miserably. Hastily, she moved her gaze to the window, pretending a sudden interest in the scenery outside. What on earth was the matter with her? Trembling like a leaf one minute, talking too much the next.

She hated Garde, she was sure she did. At the very least, she didn't like him much. But on a day like this, full of sun and sky and laughter, he was at his charming best. All she could see of him was his grin, his teasing gallantry, his strong arms holding her close. Everything else was lost.

Trembling, Lindsay closed her eyes, shutting out his disturbing image. Oh, no, she pleaded in desperation, don't let it be true. Don't let me be falling in love with him.

'It must be time to go home now,' she said, hoping to break the spell she was under.

The drive back to Eleanor's estate was uneventful at first. Jack was dozing in his seat, his small fingers curled possessively round his grasshopper toy, leaving the adults to relax in silence, not that Lindsay could do much relaxing. Her mind was hopping about like a thing gone mad. She threw Garde a slanting look, carefully, from beneath the thick curtain of her lashes. His long body was at ease in his seat, his legs stretched out in front of him, but his eyes were intent on the road. Or she thought they were! Suddenly he glanced sideways, grinning broadly as he caught her gaze resting on him.

'Have you enjoyed today?' he enquired softly, and she nodded, not trusting herself to speak.

'But I wasn't looking forward to it,' she admitted at last.

'No? Am I such an ogre to be with?'

'It wasn't you,' she said quickly. 'It was more about Jack.'

Astonishment blanked his handsome features, his expression open-mouthed with surprise.

'Jack?' he queried. 'You thought Jack was an ogre?'

'Don't be silly,' she laughed. 'I thought we were going into your office this morning.'

'Oh,' he broke in, 'now I understand. You thought we were going into my office about Jack.'

There was a short, tense silence, and Lindsay was certain the smile on his face dimmed.

94

'That's what I thought you meant,' she started to explain.

'But we don't need to go to my office about Jack,' he broke in. 'It's an easy enough legal transaction to make. All it requires is your signature.'

All! Her signature giving away her son! How could he possibly believe it would be easy! Suddenly, she could have sworn they'd slipped back in time, to that fateful day in London when he'd warned her about hurting Eleanor. He was using exactly the same tone of voice, smooth and impersonal. Her laughing companion had vanished in front of her eyes, and Lindsay took a deep, harsh breath.

'It might be easy for you,' she began.

'For you, too,' he corrected. 'Eleanor has signed her part of the agreement. She did it last night when the doctor was at the house. He and Marsha are the witnesses.'

'Last night!' Lindsay exclaimed. 'Why the hurry?'

Again, she was sure his face darkened, his expression becoming more veiled. He met her eyes, his handsome features giving nothing away.

'I can't tell you that,' he declared. 'You must ask Eleanor herself. All I can say is that she's only thinking of Jack, that he can have all Jamie would have given him.'

'All Jack needs is a family.'

'He can have that as well.'

Garde waved a lean, dismissive hand.

'No more business,' he said, his tone firm. 'Talk to Eleanor tomorrow, if you must. We agreed today would be a holiday.'

Who agreed? Lindsay reflected sourly. You and Eleanor, no doubt. Do you agree everything between you?

'But you do need my signature, don't you,' she plunged on, ignoring his warning look, 'before anything's legal?'

'Of course,' he said, 'but it will do another day.'

Well, some chance, she gritted to herself. It will never happen while I've got breath in my body.

'What on earth is the matter now?' he queried, exasperation giving his voice an edge. 'You've got a face like thunder.'

'What do you expect?' she snapped back at him.

'Expect?' he queried. 'I don't know what to expect any more, not from you, anyway. I can never make up my mind if you're being deliberately awkward, or you're just a complete and utter innocent.'

'A fool, you mean.'

Garde stopped the car, his eyes on her stricken features, and a long sigh escaped through his lips.

'Lindsay,' he said softly, 'I don't mean a fool at all. But you must look to the future, you know. Jamie wouldn't want you to mourn him for ever.'

'I loved him,' she broke in.

'I know,' he agreed, 'but maybe it's time to let go, to move forward, perhaps even love again.'

Tears trembled like jewels on her lashes. She lifted a hand to brush them away, but they only formed again and again.

'How can I?' she sighed back.

It was too much, the sad, broken words on her lips, and he took her face gently between his two hands, his mouth descending to kiss the glistening droplets away. But what began as a tender, soothing embrace rapidly developed into something more, something so sweet and deep that her heart seemed to leap wildly.

A half-stifled murmur of delight escaped through her lips as he pressed her closer, and when he kissed her again, deeply, she couldn't help but kiss him back. Involuntarily, her hands went upwards, reaching out for him, clinging tenderly to the nape of his neck.

'Garde,' she whispered, her breathing a soft rush.

Abruptly, he stopped, setting her carefully at arms' length, and without a word, he started the car's engine again.

'Enough,' he muttered, as he pulled the vehicle back on to the road.

White-faced, Lindsay fell back in her seat, hating herself for her weakness. In spite of all her fine words, she had forgotten Eleanor, forgotten Jack. Hadn't she enough to worry about already with them, without adding these hateful feelings for Garde into the equation?

After what seemed like an eternity, they drew up at the steps to Eleanor's house. Lindsay got out of the car, turning her back firmly on Garde. She needed to get away from him, as fast as she could, and his eyes darkened as she avoided his offered hand.

'I'm going in to see Eleanor,' he said slowly, 'but we'll talk over dinner.'

'Dinner?' she said, her eyes blank with shock.

'Eleanor's asked me to entertain you for dinner,' he replied. 'Marsha's expecting us at seven.'

'I don't think so,' she began.

'I thought you wanted some answers,' he said softly.

A chill feeling of dread clutched at Lindsay's heart. What was the odious man up to now?

'I thought you couldn't do that,' she tossed back. 'Client confidentiality, wasn't it?'

'I'll have a word with Eleanor, see if I can arrange something, as you're so worried.'

A haunted look crept into her eyes, and she turned away. She couldn't argue with that. She would have to eat dinner with him.

'Very well,' she agreed, 'but you'll have to speak to Eleanor first.'

'I give you my word,' he promised.

The words were enough. She didn't doubt them for a moment. Dumbly, she nodded, and then went to the back of the car. After removing Jack swiftly from his seat, she fled for the steps, but Garde's smooth voice halted her halfway to the veranda.

'Haven't you forgotten something?' he queried.

'Forgotten?' she asked, embarrassment crushing her voice to a whisper.

'Your parcel,' he reminded her calmly. 'I'll carry it up for you, shall I?'

The parcel! Of course, the parcel! Dumb with relief, she nodded her assent and followed him to the door. When Marsha let them in, she followed them up the stairs with a short commentary on Eleanor's day.

'The doctor is quite pleased with her, as long as she continues to rest,' the housekeeper finished quietly.

Garde nodded and when they reached the nursery, he left the parcel on the table.

'See you later,' he said, but he didn't smile.

'At seven,' Lindsay agreed, stepping inside.

She wasn't expecting to find anyone there, and her stomach gave a terrified lurch when Chrissie rose suddenly out of the nearest chair.

'Chrissie, you frightened me to death. I didn't think you'd be here.'

'Aunt Eleanor gave me the day off,' the girl replied, then she pulled a comical face, 'as long as I was back here in time for tea.'

'Oh, well, I can't say I'm sorry to see you. I'm all in.'

'Better get some rest, then,' the girl replied, lifting Jack out of his mother's arms, 'since you're joining Uncle Garde for dinner.'

Good grief, did the whole world know? An apprehensive tremor shuddered the length of Lindsay's spine, but she managed to raise a smile.

'You're probably right,' she stammered.

But the effort to appear calm was threatening to desert her at any second, and blindly, she made for her room before she surprised Chrissie by bursting into tears.

'Have a good time,' Chrissie's bright voice floated after her, 'and don't worry. I'll see to Jack.'

A good time? Lindsay groaned inwardly, virtually throwing herself through her bedroom door. With Garde? It was the last thing in the world she wanted. One kiss from him, and she would betray herself, betray Jack and Jamie, betray everything.

Miserably, she sank on to her bed, closing her eyes to blot out his forceful image. How could she have let it happen? How could she have fallen in love with him? A man who belonged to someone else.

CHAPTER SIX

Automatically, Lindsay showered, freshening herself after the heat of the day. She then went through her wardrobe, searching for something to wear. But one after another, she rejected the clothes she felt best in.

'This will do,' she murmured, lifting out a flowing, ankle-length dress in whispering amber silk.

She made up her face at the mirror, then caught up her hair into a soft knot on top of her head, leaving several golden tendrils floating free at her ears and the slender nape of her neck. From the drawer of her bedside table, she drew an antique locket, and fastened the fine chain about her neck. It was the only thing she possessed that had belonged to her mother. Against the rich shimmer of her dress, the small gold heart glittered like a precious jewel. She stared broodingly at her reflection, seeing the slim, lovely young girl looking back at her. But the sight brought her no pleasure. To Garde, that was all she was, a pretty child he could take advantage of, to indulge in a little casual flirtation.

Maybe, just maybe, without Garde, she might have worked things out with Eleanor. But now, there wasn't just the question of Jack

101

to sort out. There was Garde as well, and Garde made things impossible. It was all such a hopeless muddle. She loved Garde. She hadn't been able to hide it from him. How could she possibly hope to hide it from anyone else?

A knock came on the door, punctual to the dot. With an icy calm, she went to open it. But she didn't need to look to know who it was, and she was ready for him. He was standing waiting, one hand resting casually against the doorpost, and Lindsay's heart gave a queer little lurch just to look at him. He had changed for dinner as well, into a pair of immaculate black trousers, and a shirt in dark grey silk. In it, he looked a supremely attractive man, tall and bronzed, his eyes gleaming with pleasure as he looked down at her.

'Ready?' he asked, and wordlessly, she nodded.

It was clear they were going to eat alone. The dining-room was empty, hushed and quiet, the lights dim, no Eleanor and no Chrissie in sight. Even Marsha was absent, but the housekeeper had done them proud just the same. She took great pride in the running of Eleanor's house, and one glance at the immaculate table told them she'd truly excelled herself.

Apprehension was tying Lindsay's poor stomach in knots, and her face paled when she saw the spread. It seemed such a waste. She

102

didn't think she could manage much more than a bite.

'I'm not very hungry,' she said, throwing Garde an apologetic glance.

'Marsha will be very hurt,' he countered smoothly.

He took a plate, filling it with a small assortment of delicacies from the table, then he set it down in front of her.

'Try something,' he said.

'I thought we were going to talk,' she tried to insist back.

'After dinner,' he promised.

He poured the wine, filling them each a slim flute of sparkling champagne, and she accepted without speaking. Lifting her fork, she pushed the food aimlessly about her plate, unable to touch it, while he helped himself to a generous plateful.

Finally giving up, Lindsay pushed her plate aside and started to pick up her napkin. She couldn't face another mouthful.

'Some dessert?' Garde queried, pushing the fruit bowl towards her, but she opted against the fruit with a slight shake of her head, helping herself to a couple of crackers and a morsel of cheese instead.

'Another glass of wine?' he queried.

He poured it before she had a chance to reply, an easy smile on his face. Casually, he chatted about this and that, their trip to Waikiki, their walks on the beach. It almost killed her, trying to indulge in polite conversation when she was dying to ask about Jack. Any moment now, she seethed, and she would scream, at the very top of her voice.

'Talking about Jack,' she cut in firmly.

'Yes,' Garde said. 'I thought we could take him to see Diamond Head one day next week, he seemed to love it.'

Love it or not, Jack wasn't going anywhere until this was sorted out, especially with Gardener Mitchell.

'About this adoption,' she began again.

'What adoption?' he asked, eyebrows raised.

'The one Eleanor intends for Jack,' she stated fiercely.

Garde leaned back in his chair, his eyes fixed speculatively on her face.

'Oh, that,' he said. 'It may not be necessary, after all, as long as all your paperwork is in order.'

'My paperwork!'

'Your marriage lines, Jack's birth certificate, that sort of thing. As long as they're correct, there won't be any need for a formal adoption process.'

Breathing hard, Lindsay concentrated her gaze very carefully on the bowl of fruit in the middle of the table. But one more wrong word, and she might be sorely tempted to throw one of the pineapples right at his head.

'I thought we'd agreed that Jamie was Jack's

father before we came out here,' she started to protest, but Garde cut her words short with an airy wave of his hand.

'We did,' he said with an indulgent tone. 'But we need to make it official, beyond doubt, to ensure Jack as heir.'

'Official?' she prompted, a dangerous gleam in her eyes.

This was just getting a bit much. What would he suggest next?

'Just to make sure, a DNA test will do,' he affirmed smoothly, and Lindsay almost choked on her wine. 'With official confirmation of your marriage certificate, and when his paternity is confirmed and his legitimacy established, we can go ahead in claiming American nationality for Jack.'

'Is that all?' she enquired acidly.

Temper came to her aid, and these words shot out, sarcasm giving them a savage edge. Evidently taken aback, his eyes narrowed a fraction, and he gave her a long, hard look. Then he shrugged his broad shoulders.

'I doubt if anything else will be needed,' he assured her.

'I'm so glad to hear it,' she snapped.

She shot to her feet, her glass of wine tipping all over the snowy cloth in her haste. With trembling hands, she stood the glass upright again, but Garde's hand closed over her wrist as she tried to mop the liquid up with a folded napkin.

'Lindsay,' he enquired, 'what is the matter with you?'

'I thought you believed me,' she accused, the words coming in sharp, harsh breaths. 'I thought Eleanor believed me, I thought you all believed, me Now I know you don't, any of you!'

Pulling away, she ran for the door. He was calling after her, calling her name, but her steps didn't falter. Tears were beading her lashes, glittering and hot. She couldn't stay in his presence a moment longer. She made her way to the kitchen, resting her flushed cheek against the cooling glass of the window. Outside, it was a different world. There was scarcely a sound to be heard in the darkness, scarcely a movement to disturb the peace, and she sighed deeply. A walk on the beach would help clear her head.

Quietly, she slipped through the door, crossing the veranda on to the darkened sands. When she turned, Kahana House was deep in shadows, its lights burning low and bright against the horizon. She watched for a while, trying to calm her jumping nerves. Garde had brought her here with false promises, false assurances. Things hadn't changed since London.

One by one, most of the lights blinked out, leaving her alone on the dark, deserted shore, but there was nothing to be afraid of. A soft breeze coming in from the sea ruffled her hair, while the steady surge of the waves helped to soothe her muddled heart.

'It's beautiful here, isn't it?' a deep voice suddenly asked.

It was Garde, of course. He had approached as silently as any cat and was standing close by, almost invisible in the velvety, tropical darkness.

'I went to your room,' he continued, 'but when you weren't there, I came out on the beach to find you. Come back in the house,' he finished softly.

Trembling, she couldn't reply. He took a step or two forwards, and she felt his palm pressing hard against her back. He raised a hand, smoothing the wayward curls from about her face. Very slowly at first, his fingertips traced the curve of her cheek and the delicate arch of her brow.

'Lindsay, my sweet,' he murmured.

'Please, don't,' she protested, her voice little more than a sigh.

Miserably, she turned her head away. She couldn't give in, not ever again, if she hoped to keep a shred of her pride intact.

'Talk to me,' he persisted, but she shook her head.

'There's nothing to say,' she admitted.

'At least come inside,' he said. 'I don't like the thought of you out here alone,' and he pushed her gently on to the veranda.

Lindsay needed no second invitation, but

she wasn't going to run away. Instead, she looked back, taking one last look at the empty shore.

It was a night full of moonlight and stars. High above them, the moon shone down on the silvery beach, while the endless surf foamed in along the shadowy Hawaiian shore. She loved the island, every magical part of it. She loved the people here as well. But she was beginning to think, seriously think, it wasn't the right place for her. She finally walked away, pain piercing her heart like a sword. Moving into the house, she went immediately up to her room. Her head was aching, her thoughts whirling round and round. What did Eleanor want? Tomorrow, she thought, there was nothing else for it. She had to find out for herself.

She undressed in silence, and lay on top of her bed. But sleep was a problem. Like a small, hurt child, she curled into a ball and lay unmoving until the light of morning finally came. For once, she was glad to leave Jack in Chrissie's boisterous care, and as soon as she was dressed, she went down to the dining-room to see Eleanor. She couldn't rely on Garde. She had to sort this muddle out for herself.

Marsha came in right behind her, a pot of hot coffee in her hand.

'Madam's sleeping in,' she announced briskly, 'but she's asked if you'll join her for tea.'

Teatime seemed a very long way away, but Lindsay managed a weak smile. Under Marsha's eagle eye, she forced down some coffee and toast before escaping thankfully back to the nursery.

'It's Mummy,' Jack's voice called out as she came up the stairs, and a smile rose automatically to her lips.

'The coffee's still warm,' Chrissie added, looking up as Lindsay came in through the door. 'Sit down and I'll pour you a cup.'

'Oh, no,' she muttered.

The house felt suffocating, airless, and the thought of sitting still set her teeth finely on edge.

'Let's go for a walk on the beach,' she added. 'The weather's too gorgeous to lounge about indoors.'

Chrissie opened her mouth to protest, but Lindsay was in no mood to take no for an answer. Carrying Jack and hurrying the girl down the stairs in front of her, she had them out on the veranda in a matter of minutes. Helplessly, they started to giggle, suddenly seeing the funny side of their flight, but the sound of a car making its way along the drive wiped the smile off Lindsay's face. She recognised it at once. It was Garde's sleek limousine.

'Look!' Chrissie exclaimed, her eyes on the approaching vehicle, 'Uncle Garde must have finished his business already.'

'Oh, good,' Lindsay added, hoping her voice sounded more casual than she was feeling.

'I know he was going into his office early this morning,' Chrissie went on, her voice reflective. 'He said something about urgent business to complete, though I don't know exactly what.'

I bet I do, Lindsay thought, and she took Jack's small hand in her own.

'I wonder if Daddy is coming over after all,' Chrissie ventured, in a small voice so unlike her own that Lindsay stopped dead, throwing her a sudden searching look.

'Your father?' she prompted.

'Mm, Daddy is Uncle Garde's big brother,' the girl responded. 'They're partners, you know.'

'No, I didn't know,' Lindsay said, and Chrissie continued.

'Oh, yes,' she said. 'Grandpa Mitchell left the firm between them, and Daddy runs the mainland office in San Francisco. But he said he was coming over here for a holiday to see me and to meet Jeff,' then she paused, blushing very slightly. 'Uncle Garde said he might ring today,' she finished with a rush.

Lindsay smiled to herself. Chrissie's father was flying out to the islands, to meet the young man she loved. No wonder she'd wanted to stay in the house. She was waiting for a telephone call.

'Why don't you go back and talk to Garde?' she suggested. 'I'm sure he'll have some news.'

At once, Chrissie's face lit up like a beacon.

'You don't mind?' she asked.

'Don't be silly,' Lindsay interrupted warmly. 'Jack and I can make do with each other for once, can't we, sweetheart? We'll have lunch at that little diner on the beach, the one you've always wanted to go to.'

Chrissie needed no further urging. She was off like a shot across the sands, back towards the house.

'Tell Eleanor we'll be back in time for tea,' Lindsay called.

By then, Lindsay told herself swiftly, Garde would surely have finished his business at the house, and with a bit of good luck, she might manage to miss him completely. Unfortunately for her, the man himself had slightly different ideas, and after a brief word with his young niece, he came striding over the sands towards them.

At first, Lindsay tried to hurry on, chattering wildly to Jack, but in the end, she stopped. It was all too ridiculous for words, trying to pretend she hadn't seen him, since he was calling her name at the top of his voice.

'Avoiding me?' he queried as he approached.

'Don't be silly,' she dismissed, but she couldn't quite meet his eyes.

'We have to talk,' he began, but she wasn't

prepared to listen.

'Do we?' she parried. 'What about?'

'About last night,' he growled. 'I had the feeling you didn't understand.'

Didn't understand? Lindsay sniffed scornfully. Of course, she understood. He wanted to check up on her, make sure she was telling the truth, just as he'd said back in London. With a face like thunder, she walked on. However she looked at it, he had lied to her, misled her. What was there to misunderstand about that?

Darkly, Garde glared at her, his expression bleak, his patience finally seeming to snap.

'Will you stand still for just one moment?' he demanded, catching hold of her elbow to halt her progress. 'I can't hold a meaningful conversation with the top of your head.'

'Meaningful conversation?' she said, with more than an edge of sarcasm in her tone. 'Can't it wait? I was just taking Jack out for something to eat.'

She finally managed to look directly into those handsome features, but she almost recoiled on the spot. She had never seen him look so forbidding.

'Oh, yes,' he retorted, his voice like ice, 'it can wait. It can wait until tonight, when Jack's safely in bed.'

'Very well,' she managed to force out, agreeing, if only to get rid of him.

'I'm dining at Eleanor's this evening,' he

informed her, as if he was telling her something new, 'I'll speak to you then. We've a lot to say to each other.'

'I'll try,' she began again, not willing to commit herself.

'You'll remember,' he repeated, his tone harsh, 'because I'll be right there to remind you. See you tonight,' he promised softly.

'But aren't you coming with us?' Jack put in suddenly, leaping after Garde, an innocent smile on his upturned face.

'No!' Lindsay snapped before she could stop herself, and Jack's small face crumbled at her sharp tone. 'Garde's busy,' she explained quickly. 'Aren't you, Garde?'

She threw him a baleful look, daring him to say a word, but he nodded.

'Very busy,' he agreed, and he reached out to ruffle the boy's dark curls, 'but I'll be there before you go to bed tonight. I'll tell you a story.'

'Promise?' Jack queried, a hiccup in his small voice.

'I promise,' Garde responded solemnly.

That seemed to pacify the boy at last, and with a final wave, he turned to go with his mother. She took his hand, walking away briskly, and she didn't pause until she'd put some distance between her and Garde.

She made sure she and Jack had a good day on the beach, the suspicion growing that it might very well be their last. They had an unexpectedly tasty lunch of hotdogs and fries, then built the biggest sandcastle they had ever set eyes on. The sun was just beginning to dip towards the horizon when Lindsay got to her feet.

'Time to go,' she insisted, and Jack didn't protest.

'Having tea with Nana?' he queried, and Lindsay nodded.

'Having tea with Nana,' she confirmed quietly.

Happily, Garde's car had gone when they got back. The place looked deserted, and Lindsay's overstretched nerves managed to loosen a peg or two. At least, she sighed thankfully, she didn't have him to deal with as well. Only Chrissie was about, lounging in one of the garden chairs with a glossy magazine clutched in her hand.

'Daddy is coming next week,' she trilled, leaping to her feet, excited.

'That's wonderful,' Lindsay said and smiled back.

At least someone was happy.

'You're late,' Chrissie informed her, 'Aunt Eleanor's expecting you soon,' she said as she took Jack's hand in hers.

The young voice couldn't have been more innocent, but a chill ran through Lindsay's body, but somehow she forced one foot in front of the other. She could never tell how she managed to climb the veranda steps

114

without falling over.

'I'll change Jack while you take a shower,' the girl chatted on. 'You don't want to spread sand all over Aunt Eleanor's best silk carpets.'

Lindsay agreed that would never do, so it was fully half-an-hour later, thoroughly washed and changed, before they were finally ready to present themselves at Eleanor's room for tea. Lindsay went ahead, leaving Chrissie to give her a few minutes alone before she brought Jack in.

It seemed Eleanor was feeling better. The doctor had actually let her sit up for a few hours, and she greeted Lindsay with a ready smile. But Lindsay's expression dimmed. Maybe the doctor was right and Eleanor was on the mend, but her eyes were still a shade too shadowed, a measure too tired, for any real comfort.

'Are you feeling better?' Lindsay asked, concerned.

'Of course,' Eleanor replied. 'Don't you start fussing as well. My heart gives a little skip occasionally, and the whole house panics. But it's not as bad as everyone thinks. Just tell me how you enjoyed your day in Waikiki.'

It was hard, talking about something she'd much rather forget, but somehow or other, Lindsay managed to go through the day's events in a fairly steady voice.

'I couldn't really believe there was a changing of the guard,' she laughed, telling

Eleanor about Kings Alley, 'and we had a glorious sail on a catamaran.'

'So Garde made sure you enjoyed yourself.'

Eleanor smiled, and try as she might, Lindsay couldn't prevent a faint tinge of guilty colour from rising into her cheeks. He had certainly done that.

'He did,' she said, her eyes fixing hastily on to her hands.

'I'm so glad,' Eleanor said. 'I really do want you to love this place, to think of it as home.'

If the time had come to speak out, to ask Eleanor about Jack, it was now, and Lindsay straightened her narrow shoulders.

'I already love it here,' she began, turning candid eyes to rest on Eleanor's face, and Eleanor nodded, sighing.

'Good, good,' she murmured. 'I want you to be happy. I want Jack to be happy, to have everything Jamie had.'

Lindsay took a slow, deep breath and met Eleanor's smiling eyes. It was no good. She had to learn the truth, no matter how painful it was. Somehow, she forced herself to remain calm, and turning carefully composed features towards Eleanor, she kept her smile sweet and steady.

'I'm not sure I understand all the implications of this adoption,' she began, but Eleanor interrupted with a soft laugh.

'Oh, there's no need to worry about the details,' she said. 'Garde is taking care of the whole thing. He'll see that all the loopholes are safely covered, so you can leave it all to him.'

'But Jack's only a baby,' she took up her argument again, steadfastly refusing to be sidetracked. 'He needs his mother.'

'But he'll have a whole family,' Eleanor broke in, 'so stop worrying, my dear. There's no need to. Garde will make sure that everything is all right.'

'I still don't understand,' Lindsay persisted, but Eleanor turned away, a shuttered expression on her tired features.

'Leave it to Garde,' she breathed.

Sadly, Lindsay fell silent. She couldn't press the subject now, not with Eleanor so tired, and looking so ill.

'Where's Jack?' Eleanor asked, just as the knock came on the door and the small boy hurtled into the room.

'Nana,' he cried, climbing on to her bed, looking very much at home.

Surprisingly, with all the worry inside her, Lindsay found herself almost enjoying the next hour or so. They ate fresh cream pastries, served on china tea plates, and drank tea from a silver pot. Even the talk was lighthearted, with not a mention of Garde. It centred mainly on Franklin Mitchell's forthcoming visit. Even Eleanor seemed to be looking forward to that.

'Lindsay, my dear,' Eleanor said suddenly, breaking off to turn towards her, 'why don't you leave Jack with me for a while? You could probably do with a rest before dinner, and Chrissie can put him to bed after his bath.'

Lindsay's heart contracted, and her gaze flew immediately to her son's rosy face. But the boy looked so happy that commonsense finally came to the fore. Surely no harm could come to him here.

'Good idea,' she agreed, determinedly keeping her voice light, and she rose to her feet.

Fighting any desire to look back, she left them and went up to her room. There it was quiet and cool, and after the sleepless hours she'd endured through the night, Lindsay wasn't sorry to have a few moments to herself. She eased herself down on to the edge of the bed. Blindly, she stared into space. Worried to death about Jack, not to mention Eleanor, and in love with the wrong man, it was a hopeless turmoil she was in. She had to take Jack away. It was the only honest thing left to do.

Miserably, she went to the telephone, ready to call the airport. It seemed they had tickets for London the following morning. She could pick them up before the flight. Dropping the phone back on its cradle, she tried to tell herself she felt much better, but somehow, she didn't believe it. But now, she reasoned, some sleep might help. She made for the bed, legs trembling, but suddenly, sharply, an urgent hammering came on the bedroom door.

Startled, she turned, her eyes wide with shock.

'What on earth?' she blurted out.

'Please, Lindsay, please come,' Chrissie's voice came, shrill with fear, sounding so unlike the girl's usual cheerful tones that Lindsay knew at once it had to be something dreadful.

'What is it?' she exclaimed, throwing open the door.

Chrissie was standing there in tears, ashen faced.

'Come quickly,' she gabbled, grabbing Lindsay's arm. 'It's Aunt Eleanor. She's had a heart attack and, oh, Lindsay, Lindsay . . . I think she's dying!'

CHAPTER SEVEN

The corridor had never before seemed so long, so endless. It stretched on for ever in front of her, and Lindsay gave a groan, deep in her throat.

'Please,' she whispered as she reached Eleanor's door. 'Don't let it be me. Don't let it be anything I've done.'

'Lindsay,' Chrissie cried out, tears spilling over, and swiftly, Lindsay turned the handle and stepped inside.

Whatever she'd been expecting nothing had prepared her for the sight which met her horrified eyes. Eleanor was lying flat on her lack, already deeply unconscious. Her sightless eyes were staring fixedly into space, unseeing, unaware of Marsha's anxious face hovering above her.

'Come over here,' Marsha called out. 'You, Chrissie, go back to Jack. Keep him amused in the nursery. Garde has gone for the doctor.'

'Yes, yes.'

Chrissie leaped away, only too glad that somebody was taking command, telling her what to do.

Fervently, Lindsay wished that she was the one going to Jack, but obediently, she hurried to Marsha's side. Together, they turned the stricken figure on to her side, making Eleanor comfortable, keeping her airway free. That done, Lindsay took the fragile hand, stroking it gently, murmuring soft words of comfort. But it seemed like hours before the harsh breathing eased a little.

Lindsay's throat felt painfully constricted, just to look at the silent figure, and she swallowed hard, trying to ease the tears away. She was overwrought, bone-weary, almost ready to give up, when a hand fell heavily on her shoulder. It was Garde. She knew without even having to look.

'She'll be OK,' he assured her softly.

With strong hands, he eased her towards him, drawing her into the warm, comforting haven of his arms. She longed to relax against him, let him soothe her fears away, but she couldn't. It wasn't right.

'Is the doctor coming soon?' she asked, pulling away.

'Yes,' he muttered. 'An ambulance will be here at any moment.'

Lindsay went on stroking Eleanor's hand, her eyes misted over, horribly aware that at any moment, she might burst miserably into tears.

A siren sounded in the distance. The ambulance was approaching fast, and Lindsay exhaled in relief. Soon Eleanor would be in safe hands.

The family doctor came in first, his manner cool and briskly efficient, closely followed by a pair of paramedics. Within seconds, Eleanor was on a trolley, oxygen mask in place.

'Let's go,' the doctor shouted, when every dial was set and every needle safely in place.

'I'll ring,' Garde called to Lindsay, 'as soon as we have any news. Tell Chrissie to telephone her father.'

Abruptly, the room fell empty. Lindsay stood alone, in a silence so profound she could almost feel it. Trembling, she closed her eyes, trying to blot out the haunting image of Eleanor's frail form, her pale, unconscious features. Then Marsha's neat figure came quietly back into the room, disturbing her thoughts, and they listened together as the sound of the siren disappeared towards the town.

'I should be going as well,' Lindsay insisted.

'Nonsense,' the housekeeper told her. 'You have Jack to look after. You did all you could,' Marsha went on. 'It's up to the medics now.'

Slowly, Lindsay nodded. But nothing could stop the wave of pain from welling up inside her, and she fumbled miserably for a tissue to wipe the threatening tears away.

'No more tears,' Marsha murmured kindly.

That was far easier said than done. Shaking her head, Lindsay refused any suggestion of dinner. The mere thought of it almost choked her, and she sat on in Eleanor's elegant room, her eyes fixed on the silent telephone.

'It's been ages,' she said eventually.

'Not quite an hour,' Marsha corrected softly. 'They'll ring as soon as they have any news.'

Getting to her feet, she was just about to call the hospital herself, sure she couldn't bear the suspense a moment longer, when the telephone finally rang. Wildly, she leaped towards it, but Marsha was at the table first, lifting the receiver to her ear. For a time, she said nothing, listening, nodding, then she handed the instrument over.

'Garde wants to speak to you now,' she said quietly.

Lindsay took the telephone from the housekeeper's hand.

'Garde,' she said. 'Is Eleanor all right?'

'She's stable,' came the strained reply, 'but she has to have heart surgery. They're getting her ready now. If she survives the surgery,' Garde told her, 'she has a good chance of living a fairly normal life. But she's so weak, and they can't wait until she's stronger. All we can do now is hope and pray.'

Vaguely, she heard his voice promising something about ringing again, the moment they had any news.

'Has Chrissie called Frank?' he asked suddenly.

'I don't think so,' she stammered.

Surely the man wouldn't cancel his visit because Eleanor was ill. Chrissie would need him even more.

'Well, see that she does soon,' Garde insisted quickly.

'Tell Eleanor we love her,' Lindsay found herself saying and quickly she replaced the telephone.

She had no idea how long she remained there, sitting alone, scarcely aware of the shadows deepening in the room. Marsha's voice broke through to her numbed mind.

'How are you, my dear?' the housekeeper asked.

With shaky hands, Lindsay switched on the lamp beside her. She was sure hours must have passed since she'd last spoken to Garde, but one glance at the clock told her it was barely eight o'clock.

'Would you like some fresh coffee?' Marsha queried, but she bustled away before Lindsay had time to reply.

When it arrived, the coffee was strong and aromatic, and Lindsay took it gratefully. She accepted a sandwich as well. Afterwards, she went upstairs, going to check on Jack tucked up in his bed. Chrissie was watching television in the adjoining nursery, still a trifle tear-streaked, but she'd managed to call her father and that seemed to have settled her nerves a little. Patting her hand, Lindsay went back to the sitting-room to wait, but it was nearly an hour before the phone rang again, to say Eleanor was on her way down to the theatre.

It was almost dawn before the news finally

124

came through. It was all over. Eleanor was back in intensive care, her operation deemed a success. Now it was just a matter of time to see if she would pull through. Trembling, Lindsay raised shaky fingertips to brush her aching brow. A migraine was threatening behind her eyes, so she made for the bathroom. There, she snapped open the mirrored cabinet and found a foil of painkillers.

Hastily swallowing one, she hoped the headache would soon subside. She needed a clear head that morning, if she was taking a flight to London. Without Garde or Eleanor in the house, she could throw a few things into a suitcase and escape before they knew it.

For some strange reason, that didn't bring the relief she'd hoped for. The thought of going seemed to hurt even more than the thought of staying. Swiftly, she dressed in the first things that came to hand.

Without giving herself time to think, she collected her toiletries from the bathroom, and she packed them into an overnight bag.

If only Garde would ring, just one more time, to tell her that Eleanor had had a good night. Then she could slip away with a slightly lighter heart. But it didn't happen. Wearily, she closed the bag, pulling the zip shut, her heart as heavy as stone. Her case was waiting to be packed, but five minutes passed, and another five. Still she made no move towards it.

Torn by a whirl of conflicting emotions, she sank down on the bed. Leaving still seemed the better option. Surely it would be worse for Eleanor if she stayed. Finding out about Garde, about his disloyalty, would be far too much to survive. But could she do it? Garde or no Garde, could she walk out on Eleanor, a sick Eleanor, without so much as a word?

A soft knock came on the door, and Lindsay got to her feet. It had to be Marsha, but the last thing on earth she wanted was the housekeeper coming in now, finding her packing. She hadn't the energy to explain. It was easier to go to the door herself.

'Yes?' she enquired, only opening the door a fraction.

'Lindsay,' Garde said, turning his tall frame to face her.

Lindsay couldn't speak. Shock had frozen her tongue.

'I didn't think you'd be up yet,' he announced, his eyes taking in her fresh clothes, her newly-washed hair, and his black brows drew together into a dark, suspicious line. Not wasting his time on any unnecessary pleasantries, he stalked into the room as if he owned it.

He almost tripped over her case, standing waiting beside the door.

'Going somewhere?' he demanded.

The words were soft, deceptively soft, hissed with chilling intensity from between a set of clenched white teeth.

'What if I am?' Lindsay challenged.

It was time he found out that what she did was nothing to do with him. She was rewarded at once by his instant, unfailing attention. With glittering eyes, he turned towards her, his eyebrows raised almost into his hairline.

'What?' he exclaimed. 'Running away, with Eleanor still lying in the hospital. Have you no feelings at all?'

Lindsay leaped away from him, her eyes ablaze. How dare he accuse her? This man, who would happily amuse himself with her, given half a chance, without a thought in his head for his so-called love for Eleanor, he was the one with no feelings.

'I can't believe you said that,' she stuttered, outraged.

'You could have fooled me,' he snapped back. 'It's just as well she will never know.'

Never know? Stunned, Lindsay sank on to the bed, staring at him with eyes widened with fear. Was Eleanor dead? Had they lost her, after all?

'Oh, Garde,' she stammered, and for the first time, she noticed how weary he looked.

'No, no,' he said. 'Eleanor's had a good night. Everyone's hopeful. But I came here hoping to find some comfort, some understanding.'

Comfort! Her head snapped back, her expression cold with anger. She couldn't believe what she was hearing. Exactly what kind of comfort had he in mind?

'What?' she hissed. 'You honestly expected some comfort, from me?'

'Stupid, wasn't it?' he snarled. 'I should have known better. How I ever thought I might have a future with you, I'll never know.'

The ache began behind Lindsay's eyes again. She sat like a small, crushed child on the edge of the bed. He had said a future, but what sort of future had he got planned for them? Did he think she was so much in love with him, she'd be grateful for second best?

'I'm going home,' she insisted.

For several seconds, Garde didn't respond, then he turned towards her.

'But what about us?' he asked.

'There is no us,' she stated flatly.

'But why?' he persisted.

'It's Eleanor,' she blurted out.

'Eleanor?' he queried, a look of incomprehension flitting across his handsome features.

Disgust almost choked her. He was worse than she thought, talking like that, as if Eleanor didn't matter.

'I don't understand,' he continued. 'Where does Eleanor fit into this?'

'You didn't say that in London.'

Her voice was acid and he put out his hand to lift her chin.

'Are you still harking back to that?' he

128

enquired savagely. 'What else did you expect me to do? I am Eleanor's lawyer, her family's lawyer. I had to make sure you were genuine. It was my job. Was it really so unforgivable?'

Of course, it wasn't, not when he said it like that.

'Maybe I was a little touchy,' she began.

'There's no maybe about it,' he continued, 'but I had to warn you.'

'That was the trouble,' she retorted, eyes flashing angry fire. 'You were always warning me.'

'Only to make things clear,' he snapped back. 'Didn't I tell you how ill Eleanor was, that she might not survive another loss? Yet here you are, ready to sneak away.'

'Not from Eleanor!' Lindsay exclaimed, defending herself. 'I was sure we could work things out between us, Eleanor and I, if we were left alone. It was you,' she hit out. 'You were always there, trying to take my son.'

'So what?' he responded, shrugging. 'He was your son back in London as well, and you said you'd share him then.'

'Share him, yes,' she agreed. 'But not blood testing him, checking my marriage lines.'

Garde's brows rose, and sighing, he threw her an enquiring look.

'Didn't you have a word with Eleanor?' he asked, a trifle more gently.

'She just told me to leave it to you.'

'Oh, my poor Lindsay. Have you been

worrying about this all the time?'

His voice was soft, supremely gentle. Thoroughly shaken, Lindsay took a deep breath. These weren't the words she'd expected to hear.

'Eleanor is an astute woman,' Garde persisted. 'She didn't want anyone contesting Jack's place in the family, so she asked me to make sure it was legally binding.'

'And that was all?' she asked in a small voice.

'Of course! All Eleanor ever wanted was Jack legally recognised as her grandson. But it had to be hurried. She knew how ill she was.'

Abruptly, the disjointed pieces fell into place, all the rush, the pressure, and Lindsay shook her head.

'Why didn't she tell me?' she asked.

Garde put up a hand to touch her averted cheek.

'With all the pain, the worry, she wasn't always thinking straight, and when she finally agreed to let me have a few words with you, events overtook us. She had her attack, and everything else went out of my mind.'

'Of course,' she breathed, 'and now it's too late.'

It was too late. Maybe she'd been worried about Jack for no good reason, but the problem with Garde was all too real, and she couldn't see any way out of that. Slowly, Garde pulled her towards him, gathering her close, smoothing the stray tendrils of golden hair very tenderly from her face.

'Oh, Lindsay,' he sighed, 'why do you keep saying it's too late? We could have a life together, we could be happy. You know we could.'

'No!' she cried, twisting against him, but Garde was far too strong and his arms merely folded her closer.

'Yes,' he argued. 'You've led me a merry dance, my love, encouraging me one minute, snapping my head off the next. If you didn't melt so easily in my arms whenever I touch you, I might really believe you hated me.'

'I don't melt,' she retorted.

'I don't know what all this is about,' he said, 'but, my sweet, since the night of the party, when I surprised you in Eleanor's kitchen, I've known you felt the same way as me.'

'When you'd stayed the night, you mean?'

Her words were scathing, tossed out with contempt. Now, at least, he would have to tell her the truth! But maddeningly, he still tried to face it out.

'Well,' he shrugged, 'what else could I do?'

What else, she almost screamed. What else, indeed! But she kept silent, her face grim. Let him talk his way out of this.

'Eleanor had an attack that night,' he told her softly. 'Only a small one maybe, but bad enough. I could hardly go and leave her, with only Marsha in the house to help. She wouldn't let me tell you. She thought if you knew how ill she was, you might stay because you felt sorry for her, not because you wanted to. And as her lawyer, I had to fall in with her wishes.'

Lindsay remembered the slam of the door which woke her with such a start that night. That must have been the doctor leaving. Even so, it only made matters worse. Garde had kissed her, with poor Eleanor ill in her bed.

'Lindsay,' Garde murmured, 'believe me, it's all over now. Eleanor will soon be well enough to tell you everything herself and Frank will be here tomorrow. He can take care of her then.'

'Frank?' Lindsay said, puzzled.

'I know it's supposed to be a secret,' Garde said, 'but we've sold the mainland office at last, and with her surgery over and Jack's position more or less settled, there's nothing left to stand in the way. They'll be married as soon as Frank gets everything settled.'

For a timeless age, Lindsay just stood there. He couldn't really have said that. Eleanor and Frank? Getting married?

'But I thought it was you and Eleanor,' she blurted out.

She got no further. Garde moved her swiftly to arms' length, his fingers digging sharply into the soft curve of her shoulders.

'Do you mean to tell me,' he all but shouted, 'that you thought I could kiss you and be involved with another woman?'

He was really angry now. Shifting uneasily in his grasp, she stared up at him. She had been wrong about Jack, totally wrong about Garde. Had she been right about anything?

'Is that why you kept pushing me away?' he continued. 'My poor Lindsay, couldn't you see, right from the start, it was you I loved?'

The ache of unshed tears tightened her throat. She'd hoped, maybe, just a little, deep down, but she'd never known. Wordlessly, she shook her head.

'My sweet Lindsay,' he breathed, gathering her into his arms again. 'You're even more of an innocent than I thought.'

Suddenly, somehow, everything was wonderful. Garde loved her, and it was all right.

'Oh, my love,' he asked, his voice indistinct against her hair, 'does the idea of marrying me seem so very dreadful? I'll even propose on my knees, if you want me to.'

She shook her head, still speechless. The thought of the great Gardener Mitchell down on his knees was altogether too much, even for her.

'Just kiss me,' she breathed.

He took her into his arms, kissing her deeply, possessively. Then she did melt, surrendering willingly to his kiss. Gardener Mitchell really was hers.

He captured her hand, kissing its palm and each slender finger in turn.

'We can be married soon, and then we need never stop our love.'

'Is that a promise?' she asked.

'It's a promise,' he vowed at once.

*   *   *

They married in the little stone church on the hill with the sun hanging like a gold medallion in a sky the colour of sapphires. To the whisper of palms and the distant sigh of the waves on the golden shore, they took their wedding vows.

Lindsay had never seen so many people. Everyone they loved was there, Chrissie with Jack, Marsha in her very best hat, even Eleanor, still pale and wan in a wheel chair pushed by Frank. The whole of Oahu Island seemed to have come to wish them well.

Much later that evening, when all the excitement was over and they were finally alone, Lindsay lay in the sleeping Garde's arms, her head nestling securely against the warmth of his shoulder, and she gazed out at the serene beauty of the tropical Hawaiian night.

It was quite incredibly beautiful, scented and still, with the stars blazing like pale fire in an indigo velvet sky. Sighing, she stirred in her husband's arm until he woke as well.

'Awake, my love?' he murmured.

She nodded, stretching against his bronzed

frame, kissing him very softly, very gently, until his arms closed tenderly about her.

We hope you have enjoyed this Large Print book. Other Chivers Press or Thorndike Press Large Print books are available at your library or directly from the publishers.

For more information about current and forthcoming titles, please call or write, without obligation, to:

Chivers Large Print
published by BBC Audiobooks Ltd
St James House, The Square
Lower Bristol Road
Bath BA2 3SB
UK
email: bbcaudiobooks@bbc.co.uk
www.bbcaudiobooks.co.uk

OR

Thorndike Press
295 Kennedy Memorial Drive
Waterville
Maine 04901
USA
www.gale.com/thorndike
www.gale.com/wheeler

All our Large Print titles are designed for easy reading, and all our books are made to last.

DoB

✗